"Are you afraid to commit yourself?"

Justin's question was asked musingly. "Or are you just frightened of emotion? Is that why you settled for an old man?"

Cassy gasped at the way an ordinary conversation had suddenly turned personal. "We were discussing Sylvia," she replied hotly, "not me—and her father is not an old man."

"An old man as against your youth," Justin went on. "Why don't you stay here? I'd look after you. If the idea appealed to you, we could team up." His eyes pierced Cassy's shocked wide-open eyes. "Now that does shake you, doesn't it?" His voice sounded amused.

Cassy felt like shaking her head to clear the fog that had suddenly developed. She couldn't think straight. Had Justin Pride proposed to her, or not?

OTHER
Harlequin Romances
by JANE CORRIE

Many of these titles are available at your local bookseller
or through the Harlequin Reader Service.

For a free catalogue listing all available Harlequin Romances,
send your name and address to:

HARLEQUIN READER SERVICE,
M.P.O. Box 707, Niagara Falls, N.Y. 14302
Canadian address: Stratford, Ontario, Canada N5A 6W2

or use coupon at back of book.

Caribbean Cocktail

by

JANE CORRIE

Harlequin Books

TORONTO • LONDON • NEW YORK • AMSTERDAM
SYDNEY • HAMBURG • PARIS

Original hardcover edition published in 1978
by Mills & Boon Limited

ISBN 0-373-02285-9

Harlequin edition published September 1979

Printed in U.S.A.

CHAPTER ONE

'WE'RE relying on you.'

Cassy Aden looked at her uncle after this terse statement. It wasn't the first time they had 'relied' on her, she thought with a wave of dislike as her blue eyes rested on his short portly frame, plump face and small darting eyes, with the well veined nose that spoke of indulgence at the bar. She had never liked him, but couldn't ever remember disliking him quite as much as she did at that moment.

His complete assurance that she would do exactly what he wanted her to do heightened her distaste of the man, and if it wasn't for the fact that she had reasons of her own for complying with the request that she set off to the Caribbean to find and bring back his daughter Sylvia, who had gone out to the sunlit Bahamas ostensibly for a holiday but had since refused to return home, she might very well have dug her heels in and refused.

'Picked up some beachcomber, I'll be bound,' had been her uncle's bald comment on receipt of the letter from Sylvia that had stated her intentions. 'She won't get a penny out of me until she comes home,' he had added furiously, and glared at Cassy. 'And you can tell her that. She'll listen to you.'

That much at least was true, thought Cassy, for Sylvia and Cassy were very close, and whatever the reason was that Sylvia had decided to stay put, it had to be a strong one for her not to have written and put Cassy into the picture. All in all, it did rather look as if Uncle George had put his finger on the answer, and that meant that the task allotted her would not be an easy one, in spite of the glamorous setting she would shortly be heading for.

The girls were both in their early twenties. Sylvia was six months older than Cassy, and at twenty-two, should have had enough acumen to be able to make up her own mind on such matters, and no amount of persuasion on Cassy's part would serve to steer her from her course. The only thing she could do, Cassy told herself hopefully, was to have a look at the man concerned, and if her uncle was right, and if he was entirely unsuitable, then try and do something about it—but what, Cassy had no idea.

However, she had plenty of ideas on another subject and was about to voice them. 'Very well, Uncle,' she replied steadily, 'I'll go on one condition, and that is that you will agree to arrange for me to take over Mayden Kennels. You always said you would start me up in business when I was ready. I've been ready for two years now, and it is my money. I'm not asking you to back me in the venture.'

On seeing his quick frown, she hastened on, 'Mrs Peel is going to retire in a few months' time, and I want to be the first to make an offer. She knows I'm interested, and I'm sure she'll give me the first chance of taking over, but the money must be there.'

It was obvious that her uncle was not at all keen on the proposal, for the simple reason that Cassy had made herself indispensable to the Mellar family. It was Cassy who organised the dinner parties that were given to various members on the board of directors of the vast transport company owned by her uncle. It was also Cassy who smoothed over the numerous tiffs that sprung up between Sylvia and her stepmother, and as there had been no love lost between them, Cassy had to be the one to make the trip out to bring the truant home.

Mrs Mellar was ten years older than Cassy, but acted as if she were the same age, and simply refused to take over any of the responsibilities incurred as the wife of a successful business man. She loved the dinner parties and numerous cocktail parties that were thrown with depressing regularity as a get-together with the staff, and where she would receive the due homage from the younger and more ambitious members of staff. Not that she would ever step out of line, she was much too aware of her status to ever put her future in jeopardy. Cassy might not care a great deal about her uncle, but in spite of his blunderbuss way of getting what he wanted, and not caring one whit about the method chosen to gain his objective, he had old-fashioned ideas on marriage, and had taken a long time to replace his first wife, Sylvia's mother, who had died twenty years ago. Christine Mellar, the new owner of the title, was well aware of this, and being an astute woman had no intention of giving him any cause to regret the marriage.

Had Christine been the slightly nervous, terrified of making a mistake, type of person she claimed to be whenever it was time to work out the placings at a dinner table, or even make out the menus, Cassy would not have minded so much, but it was sheer laziness that prompted her firm refusal to carry out the duty that should by rights be hers. Her complimentary, 'Cassy will see to that, dear; she does it so well,' went unopposed by her uncle, firstly, because she was right, and secondly because her uncle took great pride in his dinner parties, that were a byword in the upper social bracket to which they belonged.

Apart from Christine's laziness, Cassy had nothing else to complain of, and if she had been the possessive type that took pride in running the household of a large country house, she would have been well pleased with this state of affairs, for everything went on as before the marriage, only now there was one more to cater for. Cassy, however, was not at all keen on carrying on as before. When she had first heard of the forthcoming marriage from an indignant Sylvia, she had started planning her future, a future that did not encompass running the Mellar household for the rest of her life. For her, the marriage meant freedom, and a chance to do what she had always wanted to do, run a boarding kennels.

'I'm surprised at you,' blustered her uncle. 'Talking of conditions at a time like this! If I'd the time I'd go myself. As it is, I can't. I shouldn't have thought it was all that much of a chore. You'll be seeing a bit of the world,' he shrugged his thick shoulders. 'Might even stay for a few days, once you've got Sylvia to see a bit of sense, eh?'

Cassy would have liked to say, 'Thank you, sir, very kind of you. Are you sure I can be spared?' but instead, she gave an abrupt nod and stuck to her guns. She would never get a chance like this again, and her uncle had to see that she had a right to live her own life. Whatever she owed the Mellar family for giving her a home at the tender age of ten when her parents had been killed in a plane crash, she had more than doubly repaid. Had she not been of an age to provide her uncle's daughter Sylvia with companionship, it was highly doubtful whether the gesture would have been made at all, for Cassy was only related to the Mellar family by her mother's second marriage, and was not a blood relation.

It was through this second marriage that she was able to make a stand for her independence, for she had been left well provided for in the form of shares in International Trucking, her uncle's thriving transport business, but without the sale of those shares she was unable to raise the money necessary to buy the business she had set her heart on.

'Will you see Mrs Peel and arrange for me to take over?' she asked persistently, showing him that she was not going to be put off. 'I shall be away for a week, or a fortnight, won't I? and by the time I return someone else could have made an offer and been accepted. I do know she wants to sell as soon as possible.'

Her clear blue eyes met her uncle's irritated glance; she had him in a cleft stick, and he knew it. 'Oh, very well, then,' he said grudgingly, 'but I hope you know what you're doing. It's not just a question of taking dogs in and collecting boarding fees. There's feeding, and cleaning out, staying up at all hours for collection. I suppose you've taken all that into account, eh?' he barked at her.

Cassy nodded complacently; he knew very well that she knew what she was about. If it hadn't been for Cassy's help Mayden Kennels would have collapsed long ago through lack of manual assistance, particularly through the holiday season when the boarding pens were full to overflowing. Mrs Peel had often gratefully remarked on this fact to her uncle, but it did not suit his purpose to remember any of that at this time, or the numerous occasions when Cassy would rise at the unfashionable hour of six each morning and slip through to the neighbouring premises where the kennels were to be found.

To hear her uncle talk, Cassy thought indignantly, she was indulging in a world of fantasy, and had no idea of the work such an undertaking entailed, but she did know. She had had plenty of time to witness every aspect of such a business, since she had been a regular visitor from the first day she had arrived at her uncle's home all those years ago, and had wandered into the neighbouring property and discovered the kennels. The enthralled Cassy had since made it her business to give what assistance she could, and as she was a sensible child she had been allowed to fetch and carry water to the pens and collect the feeding bowls of the doggy inmates. When she was older she learned how to groom the animals, and was allowed to give them exercise in the spacious grounds of the kennels, thus relieving the harassed kennelmaids of at least one chore. Yes, she knew what she was about all right, but her uncle would never admit it, not while there was a chance of getting her to change her mind and continue to run his household with the smooth efficiency of a born organiser such as Cassy was.

'Well, you'd better pack your things. I'm arranging for you to take the next available flight out. Pity you didn't go with her,' he mumbled. 'I'll have a word with Marchant when he gets back,' he added ominously.

'Said he'd keep an eye on her, didn't he?'

Cassy gave him an exasperated look; as he had chosen to forget her past experience in the kennels, so he had conveniently forgotten that she had wanted to go with Sylvia, but there had been two important dinner parties scheduled for that period, and she had been persuaded out of the trip on the vague promise that she go a little later in the year. On this one occasion this slight alteration in her plans had fitted in nicely with her own plans, although it had infuriated Sylvia who had been trying to get Cassy to take a holiday with her for several years. There had been the family holidays in the past, of course, when Sylvia's father would rent a villa on the Costa Brava for a month, but the whole period would be organised with precise detail on what they did each day as if there was no time to be wasted, even though they were on holiday. This was George Mellar's idea of enjoyment, and it was not until the girls were in their twenties that he agreed to allow them to make their own arrangements and choose their own holiday.

The news of Mrs Peel's impending retirement, however, had caused Cassy to regret leaving at that particular time. Mrs Peel's health had not been too good for some time, but Cassy had not envisaged her sudden decision to sell up and move into the next county where she had her eye on a country cottage. As Cassy was anxious not to miss the chance of taking over the kennels, so Mrs Peel was anxious not to miss the chance of buying the cottage, and it was this fact that made for urgency all round.

Cassy felt a surge of relief flow over her. She had stood her ground and won her case. Her uncle would not let her down; he might not like it, but he had given his word.

One week later Cassy stepped off the plane and on to the sun-soaked earth of Nassau, carrying a light coat and the small piece of hand luggage that she had been allowed to take, along with two cases that she had now to claim in the baggage section of the airport.

Her silk jersey suit that had seemed so appropriate to wear at home because of the still unsettled weather, even though it was the middle of June, now made her feel not only overdressed, but decidedly too hot for comfort, and she longed to get to the hotel she was heading for and have a refreshing cold shower.

Her passport stamped and luggage collected, Cassy stepped out of the cool airline premises and hailed a taxi, giving the driver the destination stated on the top of Sylvia's last letter home, although Cassy had a vague suspicion that she would not find her at the given address, and from then on things could become decidedly sticky, particularly for someone new to the area. However, as her uncle had often grudgingly conceded from time to time, Cassy was a sensible girl, and she had the added advantage of being able to put herself in Sylvia's position; she knew her a little too well to even entertain defeat.

The named hotel would have been the one that she had been staying at, Cassy surmised, for she had a vague feeling that Sylvia had said as much during the planning of the holiday, but that had been a long time ago, and Cassy had been caught up in the affairs of the kennels since then, and everything else had taken second place in her thoughts.

The cabby, a cheerful islander dressed in a bright

blue and white checked shirt and jeans, had taken full note of Cassy's accent. 'You from England?' he queried, flashing her a smile that highlighted his white teeth as he expertly manoeuvred the big car past the other taxis, either waiting to pick up passengers or depositing others for return flights. 'Sure is a long way,' he commented brightly on Cassy's affirming nod.

Of this Cassy was well aware, for in spite of the fact that the watch on her wrist told her that it was early evening in Nassau, her drooping eyelids told her otherwise, since it was in fact past midnight in England, and it had been a very long trip.

As it was now dusk, there was not a great deal that Cassy could see of the passing scenery as the taxi made its way out of the airport and towards her destination. Had she not been quite so tired she might have made an effort to take notice of her first impressions of the island paradise she had just set foot on, but she had to use all her will power to stay awake. She only knew she was desperately tired and longed for sleep.

There were impressions, of course, of lighted areas, and a glimpse of a palm tree now and again, and of large white Colonial-type residences, but Cassy would have plenty of time to take in the scenery later. All she wanted now was to reach her destination.

Her wish was granted much sooner than she had anticipated, for in what seemed an incredibly short period of time, the taxi was entering a long drive bordered with flowering shrubs, and soon drawing up beside a huge white hotel complex.

Judging by the activity inside and outside the hotel the cabby carried her cases into, followed by the sleepy Cassy, the place was doing a roaring business, and there was no shortage of guests. Cassy had her uncle to thank for his prompt action in booking her accommodation as soon as they had been informed of the flight cancellation that she had been waiting for, as that had been the only way she could have got to such a popular sunlit playground without having to book the trip months in advance.

As soon as the date had been confirmed, her uncle had got things rolling his end, and booked her accommodation by cable. He had left nothing to chance; there was no stopping Uncle George once he had got the bit between his teeth, and going by the influx of guests now milling around the reception foyer, it did occur to Cassy that she might find herself occupying either a poky room on the top floor, or a bridal suite, for money had been no impediment. Cassy had been given the full amount allowed for the visit, and had no worries in that direction.

However, a short while later, to her relief, Cassy found her earlier assumption wrong, and she was shown to a room on the second floor that came well up to the luxury standard the interior of the hotel had suggested. As the porter stacked her cases in the space provided just off the bedroom, Cassy noted that the unit was self-contained, for there was a bathroom tucked in behind the lobby of the room, and this pleased her, for she had a dread of wandering about in strange hotels looking for toilet facilities.

She tipped the porter the same amount as she had given the cabby, and met with the same amount of appreciation that gave her a suspicion that she might have overdone the normal expected tip, but there was time enough to get that sort of thing worked out, and at least she had not under-tipped them.

Before he left, the porter directed her attention to a printed list of numbers hung up beside a telephone on a small side table. 'Anything you need, you just ring for, ma'am. It's all listed.'

The next item on Cassy's agenda was the shower she had longed for since stepping off the plane, and although she was tired and tempted to forgo it when her eyes lingered on the comfortable bed, she searched out her toilet requirements and resolutely took the shower.

The cold water somewhat refreshed her and as she rubbed her short curly brown hair dry, she studied the list of numbers the porter had drawn her attention to. Her eyes scanned the services listed, dining room, bar, reception desk—all very convenient, and she debated whether to ring down and request something in the refreshment line, liquid that was, as she had eaten on the plane only an hour before they had landed. In the end sleep won the toss, and she locked the bedroom door and crawled thankfully between the cool sheets, too tired to unpack any other items but her nightwear. Tomorrow, she told herself drowsily, she might have to book out again. It all depended on where Sylvia was to be located.

The following morning she woke to the kind of weather one expects to get from an island in the Bahamas. The sunbeams filtered through the chinks of the window louvres, and for a while she lay and watched the pattern of the bright beams playing on the bedroom carpet.

After a short dalliance on the wonder of finding herself in such a Caribbean paradise, she gave a short sigh and jerked her mind back to her problem of locating Sylvia. Now that she was refreshed, she could put her mind to the task without tiredness hampering her mental processes. She had been too exhausted the previous evening to even ask at reception if a Miss Mellar was registered there, and for all she knew, Sylvia could be occupying the very next room to hers.

Cassy frowned on the thought. Somehow she did not think so, and was sure her original assumption had been the correct one. Sylvia knew her father a little too well to risk sending him her address.

After a light but satisfying continental breakfast, that she had had sent up to her room, Cassy searched in her luggage for a cool dress to wear, and eventually chose a halter-necked cotton dress of a bright orange hue that brought out the lights in her chestnut hair. After tidying her hair, and applying a light touch of an orange-coloured lipstick to her generous mouth, she was ready for action, and set off on her way down to reception to begin her search for Sylvia.

When she was eventually able to be attended to in the midst of the incoming and outgoing guests, all with different and seemingly urgent requests of the three receptionists on duty, and accepted with a coolness and calm that earned them Cassy's admiration, she felt almost apologetic when it was her turn to add to their harassment.

After a quick check in the register, that covered the previous fortnight, the receptionist told Cassy that a Miss Mellar was definitely not booked in that hotel. Cassy's slight nod and exasperated sigh prompted the girl to suggest that she tried the other hotels in the vicinity. There were three in all, in this particular section of holiday accommodation.

Cassy thanked her and wandered out into the spacious grounds surrounding the vast complex. Although she knew she ought to have gone to the front entrance and commandeered a taxi to take her to the other hotels as suggested by the helpful receptionist, she still had this unshakable conviction that it would be a waste of time. Wherever Sylvia had landed up, it would not be in this section of the island, and this meant that Cassy had to put on her thinking cap and try to come up with an answer.

As she walked past lawned areas around which glorious blossomed shrubs gave off a heavenly scented fragrance, her eyes saw and admired the bright scarlets and pinks of the brilliant hisbiscus, and stared in wonderment at a poinsettia bush almost reaching tree proportions, only recognising the bright pointed flowers as she had bought a potted plant for Mrs Peel not so very long ago, in an effort to cheer her up when she had been poorly.

Although she saw and wondered at the lovely kaleidoscope presented for the enjoyment of the guests, her mind was never far away from her present problem. The sun was warm on her bare arms as she followed the well kept paths that led her through the lush vegetation of the tropical gardens.

Soon she came to a sports section; tennis courts on her right, and far into the distance on her left could be seen a golf course.

It was the golf course that gave Cassy her first clue as to where Sylvia might be located. Her uncle had mentioned Mr Marchant, the firm's accountant, in whose hands her uncle had placed the responsibility of keeping an eye on his daughter. That had not really been fair, Cassy mused, as her eyes lingered on a bright red flag that directed one's attention to the green in the distance. Mr Marchant was a golf addict and had specifically come to Nassau to watch a tournament, and with luck get a game. Fortunately his wife was also addicted to the sport and had accompanied her husband, which was very fortunate for Sylvia at the time, as it was doubtful whether her father would have agreed to let her go that far away from home, even for a three-week holiday. As it was, he had charged the Marchants with the task of watching out for Sylvia— a charge that had had to be grudgingly accepted by all parties concerned, as far as George Mellar was concerned anyway, but Cassy was in no doubt that Sylvia had no intention of following the Marchants round a golf course for most of her holiday. The same went for the Marchants, who would naturally not expect her to.

Whether her uncle had taken this into consideration was doubtful, but the main thing was that Sylvia would not be entirely alone during her holiday. All she had to do, Cassy thought, was to find out where such a tournament was being held, as it was quite possible that Sylvia had booked into the same hotel as the Marchants; that way they would in part be fulfilling her father's wish.

Cassy nodded to herself. That would be the way of it. Even if Sylvia had not booked into the same hotel, the Marchants would be sure to know which one she had booked into.

With a feeling of accomplishment, she set off back

to the hotel with a light step. With any luck she would be having lunch with Sylvia and listening to an explanation of her extraordinary decision to stay in the Bahamas.

Back at the hotel, Cassy sought the assistance of the same receptionist who had been so helpful before, and made the enquiry as to which hotel would be holding a golf tournament at that particular time.

This time the receptionist was able to help her. 'Oh, that would be the Beach Hotel,' she exclaimed quickly. 'It's a little way away from here, though, in the Lyford Cay area. Any cabby will know; just ask for the Beach Hotel,' she said smilingly.

Cassy thanked her, and at her courteous reply of, 'You're very welcome, have a good day,' Cassy went in search of a taxi, fervently hoping that the kindly sentiment would be fulfilled.

CHAPTER TWO

THE Beach Hotel was an even plushier establishment than the one Cassy had just left, and considering the surrounding grounds contained a championship eighteen-hole golf course it was not surprising that the hotel lived up to the standards that would be demanded by the golf-addicted clientele.

The sport was costly no matter where it was played, but out here, Cassy suspected, it would be even costlier. Her surmises were borne out as her feet sank into the plush carpeting of the reception foyer as she went to the desk to enquire after Sylvia.

'Yes, we have a Miss Mellar registered with us,' supplied a uniformed clerk behind the impressive desk, and gave Cassy a swift appraisal as if trying to assess her business, and whether she was a friend or whether she was out on a commercial mission. He must have decided the former, for he gave her a rather bored smile and asked if she wanted her paged.

Cassy shook her head. Chances were that Sylvia might just do a bolt should she hear her name being called over the relay system, for she must have known that her father would not have accepted the situation. 'If you can give me some idea where I can find her,' she said quickly, noting the way he had flicked down a switch on a panel in front of him. 'I shouldn't think she's still in her room, would you?' She looked at her watch; it was ten-thirty.

He glanced back at a wide panel that listed the room numbers too numerous to have the old system of the room keys displayed, but they must have had some system, Cassy thought as he answered, 'Her key's not been handed in. Guess she's around the hotel. I should try the Treasure Trove,' he suggested laconically.

'Treasure Trove?' queried Cassy, frowning.

'It's a lounge,' he replied, 'first floor up. Lift's over there,' he added, indicating the direction with an abrupt nod, and turned away to attend to another enquiry.

When the lift arrived at the first floor, Cassy asked the lift attendant, a Bahamian dressed in a smart maroon uniform, to direct her to the Treasure Trove feeling slightly foolish in asking for such a destination, but the request was taken with matter-of-fact coolness, and he directed her to the end of the corridor, and to turn right. 'You can't miss it, missy,' he told her in the soft island intonation.

On turning to the right as directed, Cassy saw what he had meant by her not missing it. Instead of the usual doors to the entrance of the lounge, there was an arch-way around which hung tropical flora, and one had the distinct feeling that one had to hack away at the thick ferns covering the entrance before admittance. As Cassy moved nearer she saw that this was an optical illusion and an extremely clever contrivance to give the atmosphere the name suggested, and half expected to find herself in some kind of cavern once she had stepped over the threshold. However, when she entered she found a long sunlit room with a horseshoe-shaped bar at the far end, much like the type of lounge to be found in any other large hotel, except for the displays of tropical flowers that hung from wire baskets at various strategic points in the room.

The decor was on a theme of orange and white, Cassy's favourite combination. Cool orange and white striped loungers were in plentiful supply, as were the white-topped tables and orange chairs grouped around them.

All this Cassy noted as her eyes swept around the occupants of the lounge, and from the number of guests present it appeared to be a favourite meeting place. The talk that Cassy caught snatches of was mainly on golf, and that was to be expected, several men were dressed for action and were discussing tactics. It occurred to Cassy that either Sylvia had fallen for a golfer, or her previous tastes had somewhat changed, for her to be passing the time in such a gathering.

It was at this moment that she caught sight of her quarry sitting on a lounger not very far from the bar and talking animatedly to a bronzed man by her side. As yet her presence was unknown to Sylvia and Cassy took the opportunity of sizing up the man by her side. Judging by Sylvia's animation, and the way she tossed her fair hair back on making some point, Cassy was in no doubt that she was attempting to make some sort of an impression on the man.

He would not be easily impressed, thought Cassy shrewdly, as her curious eyes lingered on his tanned features. A strong face if she ever saw one. That strong chin of his spoke of determination, as did the finely moulded lips. His eyes, she judged, would be grey. Her glance went on to note the brown hair, not too long but cut in the style of the day. An outdoor man, she decided, for quite apart from his deep tan there were blond streaks in his hair bleached by the sun. Her

gaze then centred on his clothes, and she saw that he
wore much the same sort of clothing as that favoured
by the other golfers. So he was a golfer, she thought
with a pang of surprise. Well, that explained Sylvia's
presence in such company for a start.

Realising that she was about to give Sylvia a start,
she moved forward in the surety that after the initial
shock had been absorbed she would be welcomed with
open arms. Sylvia did not hold grudges, and certainly
not with Cassy; the girls were too close for that.

Sylvia was on the point of taking another sip from her
glass of fruit juice when Cassy presented herself with a
calm, 'Hi, Sylvia! Your papa sends his regards!'

Sylvia choked on the drink, and a few drops of
liquid slopped over from the glass that she now held
in a slanting position on to her sun dress of deep blue.
Making a swift recovery, she glared at Cassy. 'You!'
she said in low vibrant tones that would have done
credit to the amateur theatre group she belonged to
back at home. 'I suppose He sent you!' she hissed
vehemently. She flung a defiant look back at the silent
man beside her now studying Cassy with an intense
stare. 'It's her,' she said dramatically. 'I told you they'd
try and get me to go back, didn't I? Well, I'm not
going. I've just about had enough!' She tossed her
hair back and gave the man a pleading look, and
Sylvia was exceptionally good at pleading looks, as she
well knew, her wide pansy blue eyes gave her a head
start in such a situation. 'I need that job, Justin,' she
said urgently. 'Please see to it for me.'

The man remained staring at Cassy, giving her the
sort of look that made her feel naked, and kept his eyes
on her as he said dryly, 'I might at that.'

Sylvia caught his hand in a fervent hold. 'Oh, thank you, Justin! I knew I could rely on you!' she said, in a way that suggested that he had just saved her life.

Thoroughly bemused, Cassy just stood there, vaguely wondering if she ought to start from the beginning again and make another entry, as it was obvious she had come in on the wrong cue! Her indignant blue eyes stared at Sylvia, then she found her voice with a, 'What is all this about?' and looked suspiciously at Sylvia's glass. 'What are you drinking?' she asked suggestively.

Sylvia stared back at her. 'You don't have to pretend with Justin,' she said haughtily, 'he knows all about it.' She got up swiftly. 'I'm simply not going to discuss it —not here, anyway.' She gave Cassy a haughty look. 'Whatever he wants to say to me, you can tell me in my room—but I warn you, it's not going to make the slightest difference. I'm staying!' She glanced back at the man, who had now got to his feet, and Cassy noted how tall he was as he towered over them. 'Justin's just offered me a job, so I can now keep myself, and you can tell my father that I have no need of any further funds from him.' With an air of a duchess, she then ordered Cassy to, 'Follow me,' and swept out of the lounge.

'What's going on?' queried Cassy indignantly, when she had got her breath back, and they were well out of earshot of any listener.

Sylvia gave a quick glance behind her before she answered, 'Wait till we get to my room,' and Cassy was forced to do just that.

It was fortunate for her that Sylvia's room was on the next floor up, although she used the stairs rather than take the elevator. This, Cassy suspected, was a ploy to give her more time to work out a plausible answer to her extremely odd behaviour. Whatever it was, Cassy was determined to get to the bottom of it.

When the girls reached Sylvia's room, Cassy firmly shut the door behind her, absently noticing that the room was almost identical to her room at the other hotel, in that she too had a bathroom off the entrance lobby. The decor, though, was on a more lavish scale than hers.

Leaning back against the door, she watched Sylvia walk across to the bed and sit down on it. 'Now give!' she said in a voice that warned Sylvia that she had better have a good excuse for her extraordinary welcome to her.

Sylvia looked back at Cassy, taking in the flush of indignation on her high cheekbones, and the sparkle in her periwinkle blue eyes, then at her curly chestnut brown hair that framed her heart-shaped face that glinted with amber lights as the rays of the morning sun caught it, and finally rested on her retroussé nose that made her look more like sixteen than twenty-two. 'Perhaps it wasn't such a good idea after all,' she murmured, rather to herself than for Cassy's benefit.

'Well?' demanded Cassy.

Sylvia gave a low chuckle that added to Cassy's indignation. 'If you could have seen your face!' she chuckled. 'But honestly, dear, there wasn't anything else I could do.'

Cassy drew a deep breath. 'I didn't expect a rip-roaring welcome,' she said dryly, 'on the other hand, I didn't envisage quite *that* sort of welcome. What are you up to?'

An impish look appeared in Sylvia's eyes. 'You're not going to like it,' she said, giving Cassy a quick look before she went on. 'I want to stay here, Cassy,' she was serious now. 'And to stay here, I must have a job,' she explained slowly.

'I think I've got that message,' replied Cassy a little caustically. 'Though why you should want to make the stay permanent somewhat eludes me. A place like this is fine for a few weeks, but it's not home.' She gave Sylvia a long studying look. 'Who is he?' she asked abruptly. 'The bronzed Apollo you were appealing to to find you a job when I walked into the line of fire?'

Sylvia smiled. 'He's quite something, isn't he?' she said confidingly, then sighed. 'He'd never look at me in that way,' she said with a trace of disappointment in her voice. 'To him, I'm just a girl who's a long way away from home, and he's been trying to persuade me to go back.'

Cassy's brows rose in surprise; it was not as she had thought. 'Well, why don't you do just that?' she answered brightly. 'At least after this next week; I don't want to go back straight away, not having come this far, so I might as well get some sunbathing in.' She spoke lightly, for she was relieved; her task was not going to be so difficult as she had imagined after seeing the man Sylvia was trying to impress, since it appeared that he was on her side and was trying to make Sylvia see sense.

'Because I don't want to!' replied Sylvia firmly, and her glance left Cassy and lingered on her fingers now playing with the ornate tassel of her dress belt. 'It's all right for you,' she said in a low despondent voice. 'You've got the kennels, but what have I got? Apart from the office job that's becoming a rotten bore, and Trevor Bruton breathing down my neck waiting to put a ring on my finger simply because father's given him his blessing.' She took a deep breath. 'It's only through you that I've stuck it out for so long, but you've got the kennels now—or at least you will have, I can't see Mrs Peel letting them go to anyone else—and you'll move next door.' She gave Cassy an appealing look. 'And that leaves me with Christine on one side and Dad on the other pushing me up the aisle with Trevor!'

Cassy looked away quickly as a feeling of guilt washed over her. She couldn't argue with anything Sylvia had said; from Sylvia's point of view it was sadly true. Her father had set his mind on getting his daughter what he would consider a suitable husband, wealthy of course, but Trevor Bruton was a dull and rather pompous young man, and Sylvia had Cassy's utter sympathy on this point. 'He might try to push you, but he can't make you say yes, can he?' she remonstrated gently.

For this she received an accusing look from Sylvia. 'Can you see him leaving it at that?' she demanded fretfully.

'Well——' conceded Cassy, a little nonplussed as to how she could ease the situation brought about solely through her uncle's blockbusting way of achieving a target. If anything, she was rather inclined to encourage than to discourage her from her stand against tyranny, particularly as she had had to make the same bid for freedom. 'You don't have to leave the U.K., do you? Why not move in with me?' she suggested hopefully. 'There's enough room at Mayden to house a family. I'd be glad of your company.'

Sylvia flung her a pitying look. 'That won't work,

and you know it,' she said slowly. 'Besides, you wouldn't want Dad breathing down your neck every day, would you? You wouldn't have any freedom then either. He'd probably take over the kennels while he's about it!'

Cassy's small white teeth caught her bottom lip; it was a distinct possibility that he would do just that, and it was another point she couldn't argue against. As it was, Cassy was sure that he expected her to put in the odd appearance when there was an important dinner party to be arranged, but she was willing to co-operate in this respect as long as she had the kennels. She sighed. 'Very well,' she conceded slowly, 'you want to stay here. What sort of a job were you expecting your champion to find for you?' she queried, deciding to go along with her for the time being, since she was sure that the glamour of the island would soon wear off, and she would be heading for home again after a few months.

Sylvia gave her a half suspicious, yet hopeful look. 'You mean you'll help me?' she said incredulously. 'Oh, Cassy! If you're on my side, I know I can do it!' She stared down at her hands again, agitating the tassle. 'It won't be for all that long,' she confided slowly. 'I mean, I don't suppose I'd want to stay here for ever. It's just that I can't face going back at the moment. It's been so wonderful here without having plans made for me, or having to work out ways and means of getting out of one of those horribly boring weekend parties Dad's so fond of arranging, with Trevor in attendance, of course,' she added dryly. 'It was the thought of you moving out eventually that brought things to a head. I thought that if I stayed away long enough, Dad might be brought round to the opinion that I have a mind of my own, and let me do things I want to do, and not what he wants me to do—oh, you know what I mean,' she ended lamely.

Cassy nodded. She did know, only too well. 'The job?' she reminded her.

Sylvia gave a wide smile as she answered happily, 'Caddying.'

With brows a shade higher, Cassy blinked at her. 'I beg your pardon? Did you say "caddying"?' she queried.

The smile widened as Sylvia repeated firmly, 'Caddying. You know, carrying the clubs for the golfers.'

Cassy's eyes opened wider. 'But you don't know one end of a club from the other!' she exclaimed caustically.

A delighted laugh greeted this bald statement. 'Well, I do know which end they hit the ball with. What I don't know is what is which—I mean, what they would use for different strokes, but Justin will see to that. He did mention that they were short of caddies at the moment, with the championship going on. I won't be carrying clubs for the professionals, of course —er—the ones taking part in the competition, I mean, but lots of the guests here expect to have a round of golf, that's what they come for, and they also expect to find a caddy available. They pay enough anyway, and they're good tippers,' she added musingly.

The mention of golf brought Cassy's thoughts back to the Marchants. 'By the way, are the Marchants around?' she asked, breaking into Sylvia's musings of rich rewards from grateful golfers.

Sylvia shook her head. 'They've gone home,' she said, now on a sober note. 'Poor old Mr Marchant collapsed on the green a week ago, and was taken to hospital. Mrs Marchant was terrified it was a heart attack, but according to the doctor that attended him, it was a sort of sunstroke. He was so enthralled watching the golfing stars in action that he didn't take the heat into account, and he hadn't been wearing a hat that day. Even so, Mrs Marchant wasn't taking any chances, and wouldn't be satisfied until she had got him back home and got his own doctor to have a look at him. They went back yesterday, as soon as he left the hospital here.'

Well, at least her uncle could not lay any blame or charge of neglect on Mr Marchant's shoulders, although knowing him he would have a good try, mused Cassy, then brought her mind back to the present. 'What does this Justin do?' she asked curiously.

Sylvia gave a quick grin. 'To be honest, I can't quite make out what he does do,' she confided. 'He's not one of the golfers; he plays, of course, but only when someone's looking for a partner. He sometimes gives lessons on the finer points of the game for some of the guests.' She shrugged casually. 'Seems to fill in where necessary. Does a lot of organising, and knows everything that's going on.' She frowned. 'I don't think he lives here permanently. I think he moves around a lot. I did hear someone say how nice it was to see him again, and I gathered that they were residents—on the island, I mean, not in the hotel.'

Cassy was silent for a moment or so while she digested this news. The man did sound a little like a soldier of fortune, moving from one job to another, but always by the sound of it circulating the luxury circuits. Thank goodness Sylvia had had the sense to see that he would not be interested in her—or would he? she asked herself shrewdly; there was enough wealth in the Mellar family to attract someone on the make. 'Does he know your background?' she asked casually.

The start that Sylvia gave showed that her thoughts had been elsewhere. 'Oh, dear,' she said ruefully, 'now we're coming to the part I said you wouldn't like,' but a twinkle in her eyes belied her solemnity.

Taking due note of the twinkle, Cassy also noted that she had not caught on to her line of thinking, and perhaps this was just as well. She did not want to put her back up at this stage of the proceedings. 'I'm all ears,' she said dryly.

'Well——' began Sylvia slowly, then took a deep breath, 'I told him I'd decided to stay here because . . .' she shot Cassy a quick look, 'because . . .' she went on, not quite so firmly now, 'my best friend was having an affair with my father!' it came out in a rush, and on seeing the widening of Cassy's eyes at this outrageous statement, she looked away hastily and concentrated her gaze on the deep red carpet at her feet.

It was a little while before Cassy found her voice, and when she did it was several octaves higher than normal. 'You *what*?' she squeaked, closing her eyes as she recalled Sylvia's welcome to her. So that was what she had meant by, 'It's her!' 'You mean that you told him that I . . .' She couldn't go on, but stood staring at Sylvia with a look of utter incredulity on her face.

Sylvia was still unable to look at her, which was not surprising under the circumstances. 'I said you wouldn't like it,' she murmured defensively.

Cassy tried the fine old remedy of taking a deep breath, but it did not help much, and it was all she could do not to rush across the room and shake Sylvia hard, if not strangle her! 'Thanks for the compliment,' she got out between clenched teeth. 'I can only thank providence that your father's fatally attractive presence is not at the moment available!'

This produced a strangled chuckle from Sylvia, and unable to contain her amusement she threw herself back on the bed in a paroxysm of laughter.

'And what,' demanded Cassy furiously, 'was Christine supposed to be doing all this time? I suppose you forgot to tell this Justin that your father was recently married, didn't you?'

It took a supreme effort on Sylvia's part to control her mirth, but she somehow managed it. 'As a matter of fact, I did,' she replied, and on seeing Cassy's horror-struck expression she went on hastily, 'Honestly, Cassy, how was I to know Dad would send you out here? I really thought he would come himself, that's why I sent him a letter with the wrong address, but I knew it was only a question of time before he located me, from the Marchants if no one else.' She sighed heavily. 'I was certain that once Justin saw him and the way he bullies people to get his own way, he'd be bound to be on my side. You know how Dad puts people's backs up,' she appealed.

'His daughter is showing definite signs of following in his footsteps,' ground out Cassy, still partially dazed from Sylvia's mind-boggling disclosures. 'If you wanted a plausible excuse for not going home, what's wrong with Christine?' she demanded. 'Stepmothers are still in fashion, aren't they? The wicked stepmother theme is a good bet. Why did you have to drag me into your wretched machinations?'

'But that's just it,' answered Sylvia earnestly. 'You've seen Justin; he wouldn't fall for that old story, it's been too used. It had to be a bit more involved than that.' She gave Cassy a pleading look out of her wide blue eyes. 'Look, dear,' she said softly, 'no one knows us out here. The Marchants have gone home and were off the scene very soon after we arrived, so there was no one to contradict my story,' she shifted restlessly. 'And it was a good one,' she added ruefully. 'I had to convince Justin.'

Cassy's eyes narrowed speculatively. In spite of the fact that Sylvia did not appear to have lost her heart to the man named Justin, she certainly had made a great effort to impress him. 'Does he know how well off your father is?' she demanded.

Sylvia nodded complacently. 'It was part and parcel of the story. I mean, it had to be worth your while for you to make a play for him, wouldn't it?' she said simply.

'So I'm a gold-digger, am I?' asked Cassy, seething.

'Oh, I did explain the circumstances,' replied Sylvia helpfully. 'I told him how you'd been taken into the family after your parents died in that accident—at least that part was true,' she added consideringly, 'but I sort of emphasised the fact that you had no money of your own, and how hard it must have been for you when I had lots.' She averted her eyes quickly from Cassy's indignant ones. 'I also told him how friendly we were, and what a great shock it had been to find that you were ...' she darted a quick look at Cassy before ending with, 'trying to get him to marry you!'

How Cassy kept a hold on her temper she was never to know. The only crumb of comfort lay in Sylvia's reminder that they were unknown out there, and the whole ridiculous tarradiddle would never reach home.

With legs that were decidedly shaky she walked towards the nearest chair and sat down. Something that had puzzled her a little earlier now began to make sense. No wonder the man had looked at her like that! A dull flush stained her features as she recalled the look. She would not be likely to want to meet him again! She gave a sigh of utter exasperation and stared back at Sylvia, who sat watching her with a wary yet half hopeful expression on her face. 'Do I look a go-getter?' she asked with a trace of wonder in her face, 'or a scheming hussy?'

Sylvia gave her a long considering look. 'You look scrumptious,' she said ruefully, 'that's the trouble— and much younger than I do; you always have. It's your nose, I think,' she added musingly.

'For heaven's sake!' exploded Cassy. 'Why on earth was it necessary to tell such a ridiculous story? Why couldn't you have just asked for a job and done with it?'

'Because Mr Marchant asked Justin to keep an eye on me,' replied Sylvia stubbornly. 'And he feels responsible for me. I told you he tried to get me to go home, so I had to have some good reason why I should stay. You heard him offer me a job—well, at least he's seriously thinking about it, so it looks as if it's worked.' She flung Cassy another pleading look. 'There wasn't anybody else I could get to help me. Justin knows all the vacancies, and there aren't all that many, and he's got the influence to help me. Besides,' she added on a brighter note, 'they've got accommodation for the staff in some chalets in the grounds. I'd have to move out of here, of course, but I won't mind that.'

'Bully for you,' commented the still seething Cassy as she got to her feet abruptly. 'So I tell your papa that I can't budge you, do I? And that you'll come home when you're good and ready?' she asked bluntly.

Sylvia gave her a startled look. 'You're not going home straight away, are you? Oh, Cassy, you've not had a holiday yet,' she wailed.

Cassy gave her a long considering look before she replied, 'No—as a matter of fact I'm not going home yet. As you say, I haven't had a holiday, so I might as well make the most of this trip. Your father suggested as much when he was afraid I might back out of the assignment. I'll probably stay for the whole fortnight.'

A whoop of delight came from Sylvia at this news. 'Wonderful!' she said happily. 'Oh, Cassy, there's so much to see here. There's the straw markets for a start. They make hats and bags, and little straw dolls all embroidered in bright silks,' she said enthusiastically. 'I've only seen them from a distance, but we can have a good look round. I'll get one of those brochures that give guides to tourists!'

'Hold on a minute,' remonstrated Cassy indignantly. 'Aren't you forgetting something? We're sworn enemies, remember your fond greeting in the lounge just now?' she reminded her grimly. 'You wouldn't want to jeopardise your hard-earned job, would you? It's a very small island, and that Justin of yours won't relish being made a fool of. No, I'm staying, but I'm on my own from here on.'

She turned to leave, and cast a look of reproach at the downcast Sylvia. 'You can't have it both ways,' she told her gently. 'Either I'm the villain of the piece, or you own up and tell the truth—although I don't see how you can do that now, do you?' she queried dryly, and walked to the door. 'See you,' she said brightly. 'Don't leave it too long to come home, will you?' she added, as she felt a pang of remorse at Sylvia's crestfallen expression, and made herself go out of the door.

On the way back to her hotel, Cassy wished there had been some other way she could have handled the situation, but didn't see how. Sylvia had not only burnt her boats but Cassy's as well, so here they were, on a small island all those miles away from home and unable to share the pleasures offered. She felt a prick of wetness at her eyelids. Of all the situations she had thought she might walk into, she had never dreamed of one like this. Sylvia was like a sister to her, and although Cassy was younger than Sylvia, it was she who was the more responsible of the two. If only Sylvia had put her into the picture earlier when she had first had the notion of staying put, they could have worked something out, and Cassy would not have found herself in the unenviable position she was now in.

In a way Cassy blamed herself. She ought to have known how miserable Sylvia was at home, but she had taken her grumblings with a pinch of salt, for Cassy had always been able to soothe the small irritations that cropped up now and again within the family circle, bringing a touch of humour into the situation. But that was before the sudden decision of Mrs Peel's to sell the kennels, and since then Cassy had to confess that all her thoughts and energies had centred on that one target.

As soon as she had arrived back at her hotel Cassy went back to her room. She needed to think about things, and see if there was any way she could bring a little common sense into the whole farcical proceedings, although on the face of things it did not look as if much could be salvaged.

She sat in a comfortable cane chair placed by the window and took a moment or two off her problem by admiring the scenery presented to her. Of palm trees fringing a golden bay, and how the intense blue of the water turned to a deep purple a little further out. The sky was a bright blue without a cloud in sight and everything was bathed in sunshine. She gave a deep sigh as she recalled what Sylvia had said about touring the island together, and thought how wonderful it might have been, and then was back to her problem.

The man called Justin then entered her mind; she supposed it was too much to hope that he would suddenly take himself off to one of the other islands for a spell, since everything hinged on him. It did not matter about anybody else, and even if Sylvia got the job, she would have some free time in which they could do some exploring. Her evenings would be free anyway, and it was particularly the evenings that Cassy was not looking forward to. There wasn't much a single girl could do on her own once the sun had set, and she did not intend sitting in a bar lounge all evening looking as if she was hoping for a pick-up.

On this thought she was tempted to pack up again and go straight back home, but on second thoughts discarded the idea. She had come a very long way, and it would be stupid of her to back out now. Her small chin jutted out defiantly at the thought. Somehow she would manage to enjoy her trip out to this island paradise, lonely as she would be, but then she had no choice.

CHAPTER THREE

AFTER a light lunch, Cassy picked up a few brochures from the information desk that gave places of interest for the visitors to visit during their stay on the island, and went back to her room to study them and map out an itinerary for her stay, determined to keep herself busy and make the most of her impromptu holiday.

She had just mapped out her afternoon's sightseeing tour when there was a tap on her door, and without waiting for an answer to the summons, Sylvia entered the room. 'You've no need to bother with all that,' she said gaily, as her eyes rested on the brochures that Cassy had spread out on her bed. 'Justin's taking us on a tour of the town this afternoon.'

Cassy stared at her in bewilderment, then as a thought struck her, her face brightened. 'You've told him the truth, then?' she said delightedly. 'Oh, Sylvia, I'm proud of you!' she added fervently, knowing it could not have been easy for her to own up.

'Er—not exactly,' murmured Sylvia, hastily concentrating her gaze on the assorted brochures, and gave a deep sigh. 'I think I would have done if Justin hadn't offered another way out,' she said slowly.

Cassy's delight faded, and she gave Sylvia a wary look. 'Such as?' she queried sceptically, thinking that she would need those brochures after all. If Sylvia thought she would enjoy a tour of the town in that man's company, particularly after the way he had looked at her, she had another think coming!

'I tried to keep out of Justin's way after you'd left,' explained Sylvia. 'I was so miserable—it seemed so awful—you being here, and me being there ...' She gulped hastily. 'And I was trying to summon up enough courage to tell him the truth, and everything seemed to have gone wrong, so I had a good howl.' She looked back at Cassy. 'That's why I didn't want to meet him for a while—I mean, he'd see that I'd been crying.' She swallowed hard. 'Anyway, as luck would have it, I bumped into him in the lounge next to the dining room, and that was that.'

Cassy was able to feel a twinge of sympathy for her. She had felt the same way about things on the way back to her hotel, but if she had not gone overboard like that at her sudden appearance, they would not be in this situation. 'So?' she asked, still with that wary look in her eyes. She would go along with the sympathy, but that was all.

'Well,' gulped Sylvia, 'he could see that I was upset, and of course he thought it was because of you and my father. He said something about the sad facts of life,' she shrugged her shoulders, 'I don't really re- member what, as I was about to start howling again and was doing my best not to. Anyway, I said I didn't care about my father, but I did care about you, and how awful it was that I wouldn't be seeing you during your stay. I would have told him the truth then, but he made this marvellous suggestion.'

She smiled back at Cassy tremulously. 'Please, Cassy, don't turn his offer down,' she pleaded. 'I think he's got some idea of helping us to patch up the quarrel we're supposed to have had.' She gave her an earnest look. 'I think he likes you,' she said frankly. 'I'm sure he doesn't see you as the scheming hussy I described to him—or perhaps he wants to judge for himself. He does know how fond I am of you, and it's very kind of him to take the trouble to help me out, isn't it? So you will come, won't you?' she entreated Cassy.

Cassy took a deep breath; she wanted to refuse but knew she couldn't. She was extremely curious as to why such a smooth character as she judged the man Justin to be should take such an interest in their affairs, and the old suspicion reared up again that he was out for some mercenary recompense. Would he have bothered if Sylvia's family had not been so well endowed? Somehow she didn't think so. In which case, he wasn't the only one who would be doing a certain amount of judging. She had no intention of leaving Nassau before she had ascertained just where his interests lay. As for liking her—she almost snorted, he would be waiting to see which side of the fence it would be most profitable for him to sit on!

She flung an almost regretful look towards the list she had started to compose; she would not discard it, it might come in handy yet! 'Very well,' she replied, ignoring Sylvia's whoop of joy, 'but how are we to behave towards each other? I refuse to be subjected to the kind of treatment you dished out this morning, because if that's the way it's going to be, I'm staying put,' she warned Sylvia.

Sylvia squeezed her hand. 'As if I could keep that up,' she said breezily. 'No, we shall be the best of friends. It was all on my side, anyway. I let Justin talk me round, or at least think he had. He said nothing was accomplished by enmity, and he saw that you were quite willing to remain friends with me, which of course, you would be, wouldn't you? Especially if you hoped to become my stepmamma!' she added with a wicked imp of amusement in her eyes.

The straight look Cassy tried to give her wilted under this outrageous statement, and she was unable to prevent a strangled chuckle from escaping. 'Oh, Sylvia you are incorrigible!' she said, as she gathered up her list and the brochures, and tucked them into the dressing table drawer. Then she ran a comb through her short curls and picking up her bag, lifted one expressive eyebrow at the grinning Sylvia. 'Well, what are we waiting for?' she demanded. 'Take me to your leader!'

Sylvia's 'leader' was talking to a stout prosperous-looking man in the hotel reception area, and on seeing the approach of the girls he immediately broke off the conversation with, 'Ah, here's my party. See you, John,' and walked towards the girls.

Cassy felt his eyes linger on her as he walked towards them, and although his welcoming smile was supposed to encompass both the girls, she was certain it was not quite so open as his glance met hers.

'This is Justin Pride, Cassy,' said Sylvia a little belatedly, as she realised they had not yet been introduced. 'And this is Cassy Aden, my best friend, Justin,' she added quickly, as if to assure him that all was forgiven.

As Cassy's small hand was taken by the large strong brown one, she did a quick inventory of the man who gave her hand a hard shake. His casual wear of blue and white checked shirt, with grey tapered slacks and light blue sneakers, made him appear no different from any other tourist out for an afternoon's sightseeing, yet there was something about him that would make him stand out from the usual medley of tourists, and she tried to pinpoint what it was, apart from his deep tan. It could have been his haughty expression that proclaimed that here was a man who knew his way around —in more ways than one, she thought darkly, as she gave a brief nod to his casual, 'Shall we go?' and found herself shepherded with Sylvia out of the hotel and towards a large expensive-looking car that was probably of an American make.

There was ample room for the girls to sit side by side in the front of the car, and Cassy made sure that Sylvia sat next to her new-found friend, thus relieving her of any awkward conversation during the drive.

His deep well-modulated voice was pleasant to listen to, Cassy thought, as she heard him reply to several questions put to him by Sylvia about Nassau. It was not easy to identify his accent, although there were definite American undertones in it, yet not wholly so. Cosmopolitan was the word she wanted, she thought. As Sylvia had said, he had travelled quite a lot.

To Sylvia's 'Shall we have a look at the straw markets?' he gave an amused, 'You won't be able to miss them!' reply.

The road followed the coastline, and Cassy, concentrating on the sunlit vista presented, spotted a signpost that directed the traveller to the 'Love Beach', and her brows rose at this intriguing sign.

As the car followed the winding road, past palm trees whose fronds waved in the slight breeze, and the bright scarlet blossoms of the bougainvillaea of tree size proportions, it was impossible to imagine oneself being anywhere else in the world but where they were —on a tropical island, and the thought thrilled Cassy, who was determined to enjoy every minute of her time there, in spite of the bad start she had been given.

Within a very short time they were entering the precincts of Nassau, along West Bay Street, and finally into Bay Street. The distance could not have been much more than four miles, Cassy surmised, and this made everything nice and handy for her if she found herself on her own, and judging by the quick surreptitious looks she received every now and again from the man at the wheel, this was more than just a possibility. It was odd really, she mused, that although he had made an effort to talk Sylvia round into taking a more understanding view of what was supposed to be her best friend's mercenary intentions, Cassy had a feeling his own view would not be quite so liberal. Of course, if he was just a kindly man out to help a girl in trouble, then Cassy would applaud these sentiments and be only too happy to bow out of the scene, no matter what Sylvia said. She was even agreeable to accepting the label of 'go-getter' under these circumstances, particularly if Sylvia was able to land herself a job. However, as things stood, Cassy was not yet convinced that the man's intentions were wholly altruistic.

As the car glided along the main thoroughfare of the capital of New Providence, Cassy determinedly thrust all these thoughts aside and concentrated on the tour of the city. Her eager eyes skimmed the tree-lined road bathed in sunshine. Here again, palm trees intermingled with other trees that she could not identify. White and pink stone buildings loomed up in front of them, and on either side of them could be seen the shopping areas. The traffic here was denser than it had been before, and Cassy noticed that it was the same as in England, as far as traffic rules prevailed, for they were driving down the left side of the road.

'Look, Cassy,' exclaimed Sylvia, 'there's a horse-drawn carriage—and look at that straw hat the horse is wearing—isn't it gorgeous! I want to get a straw hat myself.'

'We can take one of the carriages for part of the tour,' remarked Justin. 'As for buying a hat, you'll be spoilt for choice in a minute,' he added in an amused tone, as he guided the car into a parking space by a lawned square surrounded by palm trees.

As they alighted, Sylvia squeezed Cassy's arm in a manner that showed her happiness at her presence, and her eager anticipation of the tour. Cassy only hoped that this happy state of affairs would prevail, but she had an odd sensation that it was not going to be as easy as that.

'Did you say you wanted a hat?' queried an amused Cassy a few minutes later, as they looked at stall after stall of straw millinery wear, and not only hats. There were bags, handbags, straw donkeys of toy size, and tiny dolls, some dangling from string in the front, and at the side of the stalls, and others lined up on the ground in rows.

The brilliant colours of the silks woven into each article was the first thing that caught the eye. No matter how small, and some of the dolls were very small, all were embroidered with the rich gay silks. Even the tiny straw hats sported by the toy donkeys had been industriously decorated.

The happy chatter that came from the numerous stallholders as they vied for custom from the milling crowd of tourists searching for bargains, and bartering for some special item that had caught their eye, added atmosphere to the scene. As for the hat Sylvia had said she wanted, she was indeed spoilt for choice, the only difficulty being which type to choose. Cassy rather favoured the same type as the plump, smiling stallholder was wearing, and that was a Chinese coolie style with a bright blue flower woven into the conical shaped crown.

In the cool recesses of the stalls, the women could be seen at work weaving the wares they sold. It was a happy thriving industry, that almost made Cassy envy them their industrious but easy-going life. Trade was good, in spite of the numerous stalls to choose from, for there was enough custom for all to get a fair share of trade. As Justin explained to the girls, apart from the usual tourists who spent their vacations there, there were the visits of the cruise ships that tied up in port at least twice a week, and landed passengers for inland tours and shopping sprees.

As he spoke Cassy's gaze went over his strong features and she noted that she had been right in thinking that his eyes were grey, a bluish grey that would probably alter with his mood, and again it struck her that for a man of his stamp he was taking an extraordinary interest in Sylvia's fictitious story. Her glance lingered on the gold watch on his wrist. A strong wrist, she thought idly, as she saw how the sun had bleached the hairs on his wrist that overlapped the gold link-chained strap.

'I think you ought to purchase a hat, too,' suddenly

remarked the man Cassy had been covertly studying, and she came to with a start when she realised that he was referring to her.

'There's an orange embroidered one that would suit you, Cassy,' said Sylvia. 'Come on; you get that one, and I'll get the blue one next to it. Justin's right, it does get hot here, and we don't want to land up like poor Mr Marchant, do we?'

Cassy allowed herself to be pulled over to the stall from which Sylvia had spotted the hat she thought might suit Cassy, and even though the next few minutes were spent in good-humoured bargaining for the required hats, Cassy could not rid herself of a feeling that the man had been perfectly aware that she had been mentally summing him up, and it gave her a sharp jolt. She hadn't been that obvious, had she?

After the girls had made their purchases and emerged mistakenly triumphant with what they had presumed to be a bargain, Justin pointed out that they could have got a better price, but at least justice had been done on all counts, and all parties were satisfied.

On Justin's light, 'Ready to move on?' both girls nodded assent, and followed his tall back out of the market and through to an arcade supported by white stone pillars. 'This is Sunley Arcade,' he said, 'if there's anything else you need.' He glanced again at Cassy, and again she wondered why he had to confine his remarks to her. 'Such as sunglasses,' he suggested, 'or whatever, you'd better purchase them now, we'll be moving out of the town section after this.'

'I've got my sunglasses,' remarked Sylvia. 'I expect you have too, haven't you, Cassy?' she asked, then added swiftly, 'But we would like a peep at the shops, if you don't mind, Justin? Wouldn't we, Cassy?' she appealed to her.

Cassy was not too sure about this, she felt that enough time had been taken up already on the purchase of hats, and was sure the man had a host of other things he would rather be doing than escorting a couple of wide-eyed tourists around the island. 'We can come shopping another time,' she said hastily. 'It's not as if it's far to come, everything's so handy.' To be strictly honest, she hoped the man would agree, and that they would get the tour over with as quickly as possible and the girls would be left to their own devices, and only then could she really begin to enjoy herself.

'We've plenty of time,' he answered casually, dashing any hopes Cassy had had of a swift tour, and the quick almost assessing look he gave her told her that he was aware of her sentiments. 'It's part of the tour. There's quite a lot of interesting wares for sale that are confined only to the islands, as you'll see,' he remarked, as he led them into the bright sunlit arcade, made brighter after the short walk through the shady covered entrance to the arcade.

The minute they entered the square, all thought of shopping was temporarily thrust aside as the girls gazed in delight at the large fountain in the centre of the arcade, in the shape of a swimming pool, out of which rose two life-sized bronze statues, of a man and a woman, with the man leading the way with arms outstretched as if about to take wing out of the pool, and into the blue horizon, followed closely by the woman whose arms were raised in the same pose of glorious unfettered freedom. The illusion was completed by the leaping bronze dolphins that played around the edge of the pool. The sparkling spray of the fountain seemed to bring the scene to life, and the girls were entranced.

In spite of the ample size of the fountain, there was plenty of room to walk around it and gaze into the windows of the shopping area that surrounded the fountain. There was greenery too, in the form of the same sort of trees that had lined the street they had passed through as they entered the capital, and as Cassy's eyes dwelt on the small light green leaves, she felt uplifted, and was even able to look kindly on her Uncle George for making her take the trip out there, for she doubted that she would ever come again.

As far as shopping went, there was plenty of choice, including one store that proudly called itself, 'The Dollar Shop', and offered many wares at the named price. Whatever might be required, Cassy was sure would be catered for in that one confined courtyard, although there were many shopping areas around the city, she doubted whether the setting would be quite so pleasant, for one could always sit by the fountain and watch the other tourists searching for bargains in that busy yet relaxed atmosphere.

There was one item that Cassy had forgotten to bring, and that was a camera, but she hoped to be able to purchase some slides of each area visited before she returned home—and that should not be too difficult, she thought, as her eyes rested on a stand full of bright postcards showing various island scenes; she could always purchase a few of those if slides were unavailable.

Perfumery shops were plentiful, and claimed the girls' attention, particularly where prices were concerned, for all the known makes were prominently displayed, and after working out the dollar exchange rate, they realised that there were plenty of bargains to be had.

A peep into another shop called 'The Treasure Box' showed displays of pale pink jewellery made out of conch shells, and delicate necklaces of crushed coral. There were brooches and rings, also of crushed coral, that shimmered in a kaleidoscope of colour; soft reds, yellow, pink and black, not unlike a rainbow. Sylvia let out a gasp of pure delight as she spotted a gorgeous coral brooch shaped like a dahlia, the irradiance of the coral making it appear a living flower. Jewellery fascinated Sylvia, unlike Cassy, who only wore it when the occasion demanded, and even then only the barest amount.

Amidst Sylvia's exclamations and frequent clutching of Cassy's arm when something caught her attention, Cassy found time to wonder at the patience shown by their escort, who now and again would make some comment, and did not seem at all embarrassed by the enraptured Sylvia. In all probability, she mused silently, he had done this sort of thing before, perhaps filled in as a guide to the better endowed visitors to the island. He had said something about it being part of the tour, hadn't he?

At this point Sylvia made another discovery. 'Oh, look, Cassy! They even make jewellery out of coconut shells!'

'It has to go through several stages before it's ready for sale,' commented Justin. 'The fibre must first be removed, and then it's sanded and brushed. If it has to have a design, painted on it, such as that brooch there,' he indicated a beautifully painted piece of jewellery, 'then that part of the shell has to be smoothed, and heat and varnish is applied before the design is painted on it. It's a lasting gift though, very durable.'

They had moved on a few paces from the shop when Sylvia suddenly said, 'Wait here, I won't be a moment,' and disappeared into the jewellery shop they had been looking at a moment ago.

Cassy had a nasty feeling that she knew what Sylvia's intention was. It was more or less obvious by the way she had made them walk away from the shop, and then slipped back on her own. Only too well did she know her penchant for doing something on the spur of the moment, and this time Cassy was sure she was about to buy something for her, as she could not envisage her buying their escort any such gift.

Her suspicions were confirmed a moment later when Sylvia joined them and thrust a little package into her hand. 'I couldn't resist buying them for you, Cassy,' she said happily. 'I know you don't often wear earrings, but these are the same orange colour you're so fond of.'

Highly embarrassed, Cassy wanted to slap Sylvia for her thoughtlessness. She had entirely forgotten that they were supposed to be at loggerheads with one another, and even if a temporary truce had been called, one did not buy such gifts for someone one considered a traitor.

There was another side to consider, of course, and one that had not occurred to Cassy, but that had definitely occurred to Justin Pride, and it was not long before she was acquainted with this fact.

'Shopping over?' queried Justin, with one eyebrow

raised in query at Sylvia after she rejoined them, and received a firm nod from both girls, but a more emphatic one from Cassy. 'Good, well, we'll start with the tour. I think we'll take in the Queen's Staircase next. I expect you've heard of that?' he asked, yet his query was more confined to Sylvia than to Cassy, and she wasn't sure whether it was her imagination or not, but she sensed a kind of reserve behind his quick glance in her direction, that might have been there earlier, but if so, she had failed to detect it.

At this thought she felt a surge of resentment flow through her. Whatever she was supposed to have done, it was none of his business. Judging from what Sylvia had told her about his way of life, he was hardly in a position to judge, was he? she asked herself furiously. The sooner this tour was over, the better, she told herself, and no matter what Sylvia had in mind for future tours, if they included this man then she would cry off. They could always pretend that they had had another row, couldn't they?

They walked along Bay Street, and turned into an avenue called Elizabeth Avenue, and across another street, and eventually found themselves in a cool section of the city. The way to the Queen's Staircase was along a pathway cut out of sheer rock, as was the staircase itself.

On either side of them loomed the steep sides of the solid rock limestone from which sprouted ferns of a light emerald green, and relieved the otherwise grim face of the reddish-brown stone. At the sides of the path grew palm trees and other plants, making the whole scene represent an oasis in the middle of the thriving city. Yet even here the straw sellers had their markets, and several stalls were set up at the side of the road.

The bright colours of their wares gave a carnival atmosphere to the proceedings, and a gaily painted landau, drawn by a horse decked out with what looked like a spray of flowers on his head, completed the scene. 'Shall I see if he's hired?' asked Justin. 'We could finish the rest of this afternoon's tour with him, if you like.'

However, before the driver could be approached another party of tourists beat them to it. 'Oh, never mind, Justin,' said Sylvia. 'To be honest, I'd rather walk—well, as far as we can, anyway, wouldn't you, Cassy?' she asked, and received an absentminded nod from Cassy who was staring up at the steps ahead of them. Sixty-five in all, and carved out of the rocks by slaves, and Sylvia, following her glance, shivered. 'Who said, "the good old days"?' she queried, and turned to Justin. 'They're called the Queen's Steps after Queen Victoria, aren't they? Something to do with the abolition of slavery, wasn't it?' she asked him.

Justin smiled at her. 'I see you've been doing your homework,' he said. 'Yes, that's so, but the steps were originally carved to give the garrison troops a quick getaway from Fincastle Fort. We'll take a look at the fort next. These are not the original steps, by the way, as you can see they have since been replaced.'

As they neared the steps, a small waterfall was seen at one side of the steps, and seeing Cassy's eyes lingering on it, Justin remarked, 'It shows up much better at night, they floodlight it.'

They ascended the steps and several times had to move swiftly aside to avoid getting in the way of the numerous camera shots that were being taken by other tourists from the top of the steps, and also from the bottom.

'No cameras?' quizzed Justin, as they once again moved aside to avoid ruining a picture.

'I've left mine at the hotel,' wailed Sylvia. 'Still, I expect we can always come back again at some other time,' she added hopefully, and looked at Cassy.

Cassy however, was not yet ready to commit herself on any further tours, be it a revisit to the one they were now taking, or any other tour, not unless they went on their own, and in that case she had no objection.

When they arrived at the top of the steps, they stopped to admire the view of the cool passageway through the rocks that they had just walked through, and Sylvia, who had moved aside from them in order to get a better view, found herself approached by a couple of American tourists who asked if she would mind taking a snap of them on the steps, and she cheerfully obliged, taking not only one, but several, in different poses with the Queen's Staircase in the background for the grateful couple.

Cassy and Justin stood aside and watched the proceedings, Justin with an indulgent air, and Cassy with a slightly worried one, for she hoped Sylvia had remembered to include the heads of the couple in the snaps as well as the feet, having had some experience of such catastrophes in the past with Sylvia's enthusiastic if not very brilliant photography.

'Is it going to be worth it?' asked Justin, in a low voice that only Cassy could hear, and she was jerked out of her musings with a start as she tried to work out whether he was referring to Sylvia's photographic efforts or to some other matter, and she was left in no doubt when he added, 'Surely there are other ways of making your fortune without hurting someone who's as fond of you as she is.' He did not look at her as he said this, but at Sylvia, still happily engrossed in her voluntary task.

Cassy stared at him, then blinked as the full implication of what he was saying hit her. She drew in a deep breath before she answered, 'I fail to see what it's got to do with you—and I have no intention of discussing our private business with a stranger,' she added haughtily, wanting to shout out at him that it wasn't her fault if he had been stupid enough to believe the story Sylvia had told him.

'I might be a stranger now,' he said, still in that low yet penetrating voice, 'but you're going to know me pretty well before you leave—I can promise you that,' he threatened.

Sylvia joined them before Cassy could reply to this extremely provocative statement, and this was just as well since she was having a hard time believing the evidence of her own ears, and could have been forgiven for thinking she had imagined the whole episode. One thing she was certain of, and that was that she would make certain that she was never alone with this man again, even if it meant chaining Sylvia to her side for the rest of the tour!

CHAPTER FOUR

CASSY listened to the short history lesson being given by Justin Pride on the small fort they were now looking at, and found great difficulty in keeping her mind on the salient facts being pointed out. Afterwards, all she could recall was the lovely view from the fort to the bay beyond, and a glimpse of several luxury liners anchored there.

'Like the other two forts around the city,' went on Justin's voice breaking into her musings, 'not one of those cannons was ever used. The threatened invasion never took place.'

All this Cassy heard, without any of the narration really penetrating her thoughts. He could have been giving a lecture on some kind of Swiss cheese for all the attention he was getting from Cassy, and her eyes remained fixed on the panorama before her.

Although her eyes rested on the blue of the bay and the delta-like ridges on which bright greenery grew, and on to the elegant lines of the luxury ships, her whole being was centred on the short but highly charged interchange she had had with the man now answering Sylvia's questions.

It was as well for Cassy that Sylvia was taking an interest, and she did not know what she would have done if Sylvia had directed any attention back to her, but fortunately she had noticed nothing unusual in Cassy's reticence.

Above the natural resentment she felt at the man's unasked-for intervention, not to mention the charge he had laid at her door, of her seeming selfishness in obtaining her goal regardless of Sylvia's feelings, she knew a deep sense of hurt that anyone could accuse her of such machinations. She had been made to feel a thief stealing a slice of fortune that rightly belonged to someone else, and it was of no avail reminding herself that she was a victim of Sylvia's fertile imagination. Had her accuser been anyone else but this censorious male, she doubted if the farcical situation would have affected her in quite this way.

Her feelings were so acute at this point that she was very much inclined to enlighten him as to the true state of affairs, and only just prevented herself from doing so on the thought that it was, after all, a selfish wish on her part, and although Sylvia had done a stupid thing, she had to concede that she had been partly responsible in forcing her to take such an action.

She drew an inward sigh of frustration at the thought that none of this would have happened if she had not been so taken up with her own affairs, and had not let the kennels take precedence over all else, including Sylvia's unhappiness at the sort of life she was leading. She straightened her shoulders. Well, she would have to put up with the consequences now, it was the least she could do, and why she should let this autocratic specimen's opinion influence her like this, she did not know.

Her brooding eyes left the scene in front of her and rested on Justin as he smiled at something Sylvia had said, and she noted how white his strong even teeth were against his deep tan. Oh, he was attractive, all right, and she could imagine his success with the opposite sex; they would positively hang on to his every word—as much, she thought sardonically, as Sylvia was doing at that very moment, even though she had no idea that she was behaving like a moonstruck female —such was the man's attraction. It might also, she admitted unwillingly to herself, be the reason why she so wanted him to look kindly on her, and not look on her as a kind of parasite that had latched itself on to the money waggon.

The thought somewhat shook her, and she firmed her lips together. It was not like her to be taken in by a handsome face, it was what was behind the façade that mattered, not what was on the surface. At this point her brooding eyes met his, and brought home his astounding prophecy of her getting to know him better before she left the island. To her utter consternation, she felt herself flush under the gaze of those relentless eyes of his, and wished the ground would open up and swallow her.

'Next stop, the Water Tower,' he said, as he shepherded the girls down the short flight of steps that led to the fort, and Cassy wished miserably that she could somehow lose herself among the jostling crowd ascending and descending the same steps.

For the rest of that afternoon's tour Cassy might just as well have been back at the hotel for all the notice she took of the remainder of the tour. Seeing yet not seeing the wonderful panoramic view from the top of the Tower that overlooked the whole island, she promised herself grimly that she would come again, as she felt a spurt of resentment against the man who had so successfully ruined what might have been a wonderful start to her island holiday.

When at last a halt was called, and a suggestion of going back to the hotel for tea was made by Justin, Cassy tried to come up with an excuse as to why she should not accompany them back to their hotel, but could not think of a good enough one, apart from being blatantly honest and declaring that she had had enough of Justin Pride's company for one day, and she had to go along with the suggestion, but her moody blue eyes said more than words when they met the challenging grey ones of the cause of her discomfort.

There was, however, just one tiny consolation, and that was that the afternoon's tour was over, and she could in all justification leave after tea and return to her own hotel, where, she promised herself fervently, she would stay for the rest of the day. If Sylvia was going to be on her own for dinner, and this was quite likely, she thought, as she was sure the extremely busy Justin Pride would have his own plan of amusement for the evening's entertainment, then she would suggest Sylvia come over to her hotel for dinner.

With this firm resolution in mind, it was disconcerting for Cassy to find that she was given no choice in the matter whatsoever, and her planned retreat was quite definitely baulked. Her attempt at a hasty departure directly after tea, with a, 'Well, I must get back to my hotel. I haven't unpacked properly yet,' met with an equally casual, 'We'll pick you up at eight,' from Justin, who had stood up when Cassy had, fully intending to run her back to her hotel.

The thought of even that short ride in his company was more than Cassy was prepared to take, and

she assured him that she could get a taxi, there were
plenty to be had. With that hurdle out of the way, she
made a stand against the next one, and excused herself from whatever Justin had in mind for that evening. 'I think threesomes are boring, don't you?' she
remarked lightly to him, with a look that told him that
she would prefer to be on her own, but she need not
have bothered!

'Oh, that's no problem,' he answered, in the tone of
voice that told her that she was on a losing streak.
'We'll make it a foursome,' making Cassy want to
hurl the cream jug at him. His added rider of, 'Evening dress, by the way,' increased her resentment of
him, but did give her a ray of hope.

'Then you'll have to excuse me,' she said triumphantly, 'I've no such garments with me.'

'Oh, you can wear one of mine,' broke in the ever
helpful Sylvia, for which she received a baleful glance
from Cassy. 'We're the same size, aren't we?' she went
on, quite unperturbed by the look Cassy sent her. 'The
white one will suit you—you know the one I mean,'
she added confidently, and a fuming Cassy had to
accept the situation.

The dress Sylvia had so kindly lent Cassy was of a
fine lacelike material with an underskirt of silk, and
very definitely suited Cassy's chestnut colouring, although she was totally unaware of this as she gave
herself a last-minute check in the mirror before going
down to the lounge to await the threatened collection.

Her deep blue eyes flicked unemotionally over her
reflection, noting how the line of the dress clung inti-
mately to her figure, and how, even though she was
about an inch taller than Sylvia, it nicely covered her

ankles, leaving her ample space for either walking or
dancing. As to the latter, she could wriggle her hips
and beat time to the music, which appeared to be all
that was required in the modern fashion, but as far as
the actual art of dancing went, she didn't have a clue.
Cassy had never had cause to regret this state of affairs
before, but it certainly would have been a help if she
could dance, for it might have been one way of releas-
ing her from Justin Pride's company—always assum-
ing her partner, whoever he was, was of an energetic
nature.

A glance at her watch told her that it was time she
put in an appearance in the lounge, and she picked up
the white lace shawl Sylvia had thoughtfully provided
her with to go with the dress, collected her handbag,
and after locking her door, made her way down to the
lounge.

Any hope she might have harboured that there
might have been a change of plan, or that Sylvia had
a headache and had cried off, or that Justin Pride's
august presence was required elsewhere, were quickly
dashed by the tall form of the man himself as he un-
folded his long lean length out of the chair he had
accommodated to await her arrival.

Cassy took her time in walking towards him, feeling
very unsure of herself, and the flutter she felt in her
heart region was purely and simply nerves, she assured
herself stoutly, although she had thought him handsome before, but now, dressed in full evening regalia,
he was outstanding. That she was not the only one of
this opinion was borne out by the stir of interest from
a group of women at the end of the lounge, either
waiting for their menfolk to desert the bar and join

them, or out for an evening on their own.

Her veiled eyes gave none of her thoughts away as he casually caught her elbow in an action that spoke of possessiveness as they walked out of the lounge and out of the hotel to the waiting car without a word being spoken. In spite of Cassy's determination not to be overawed by this man's presence, she felt a spurt of feminine pride as she caught the wistful looks sent in their direction from the other women.

By now night had fallen. Sunset, to Cassy's surprise, had been around seven-thirty, which was early by English time standards. When they reached the car Cassy, seeing Sylvia sitting in the back of the car, started to join her, but Justin directed her to the front seat beside him, and for a moment she hesitated before complying, then as she took her seat she found that the space beside Sylvia was occupied by a young man who leaned forward with a, 'Hi!' greeting to her.

As she returned the greeting, Cassy felt slightly foolish, but it was not her fault that his dark evening suit had concealed his presence. She did wonder, however, why he was sitting in the back with Sylvia when he was supposed to be her date for the evening.

'This is Greg Storn, Cassy,' said Sylvia, introducing them. 'He's going to teach me to play golf, so I'll know what's what,' she added lightly on an amused note.

Unfortunately Cassy could derive no amusement from this news, since she was beginning to develop a very unwelcome premonition as to who her partner was going to be for that evening, and by the time they had arrived at the Bridge Inn, the hotel Justin had chosen to take them for dinner, she had the answer!

He had already ruined her afternoon's sightseeing tour, she thought bitterly, so he might as well make a day of it by ruining her evening as well, she told herself in a vain attempt at jocularity to minimise her disappointment. The infuriating thing was that she had had no choice in the matter, since it was obvious that Greg Storn and Sylvia were acquainted with one another.

From then on Cassy had no expectation of an enjoyable evening, although Sylvia had every expectation, for her escort, a tall blond, healthy-looking young American, was more than just interested in her, and was touchingly shy about it, making his interest a nice change from the usual brash approach adopted by so many males.

The panoramic view from the outdoor dining patio of the hotel, that was situated opposite Paradise Island Bridge, would have been so much more appreciated by Cassy under any other circumstances, but as it was she gazed out at the palm-fringed bay lit by floodlighting, and beyond that to the star-filled sky, feeling cheated once again out of what might have been a wonderful experience.

Considering her feelings, it was not surprising that she took little interest in the subject of food, and the menu handed to her by Justin received scant attention, and she handed it back to him saying in a voice devoid of emotion, 'I'll leave it to you.' Afterwards she wished that she had stipulated that she was not too keen on 'fried squid with garlic sauce', neither would she appreciate 'turtle steak'!

As far as food was concerned it appeared her luck was in, for Justin ordered steaks, and something called 'peas and rice', that sounded an unlikely combination, but was a Bahamian speciality.

The peas were pigeon peas, and not the familiar type of garden peas used at home, and reminded Cassy of the sultana flavouring in curries made at home. She would have liked to have made a few enquiries as to where the name derived from, but was in no mood to make conversation, for the question would have to be asked of Justin, as Sylvia and Greg were indulging in a gay exchange of quips on golfing terms.

The sweet was another Bahamian speciality and was called 'Bahamian Ambrosia', consisting of pineapple, mangoes, bananas and cherries, with shredded coconut mixed in ginger ale, and was highly palatable, even to Cassy's slightly depressed taste buds.

In spite of Cassy's reluctance to indulge in conversation, the foursome was a gay one to all other intents and purposes, and Justin was soon assisting Greg in initiating Sylvia into the mysteries of golf, and seemed content to let Cassy play a minor role in the proceedings. It was only when Sylvia called her attention to a happening some time ago that involved her father that Cassy felt his interest stray from the subject of golf and concentrate on her, and by the way his eyes slightly narrowed as they rested on her, she could almost sense his thoughts, and longed for the end of the evening.

When dinner was over Cassy found her ordeal was only just beginning, as the strains of dance music drifted towards them from the hotel, and Greg asked Sylvia if she would like to dance. To Cassy's consternation, she accepted with an eagerness that made Cassy wonder how she could have been so cruel as to leave her stranded with Justin.

Justin asked her if she would like to dance, too, and the look he sent her when she gave a swift, 'no', made her hastily explain that she was not much good at it, and how she would hate to embarrass him.

'There's not much chance of that,' he replied dryly. 'All you have to do is follow my lead. Well?' he challenged her with a mocking look in his eyes.

The next moment Cassy found herself being escorted to the dancing area, wondering just how he had managed to manipulate even this small victory, and that she had a lot to learn about this enigmatic man.

'One quick step, and then two,' said Justin, when a few minutes later she found herself in his arms amidst a throng of dancers.

Any hopes that she might have been secretly nursing that he might fall over her feet, that were bound to be in the wrong position at the right time, were soon diminished by his expert guidance, and her feet glided into the rhythm of the dance with surprising expertise.

So much so that Justin was prompted to drawl, 'You learn fast,' and made her miss the next step as she searched for the underlying meaning in his words, and stared up at him with a wary look in her eyes.

'I meant dancing,' he added, with a touch of irony in his voice, and drew her nearer as he corrected their steps.

From what had been a reasonable distance between them, he was now a little too close for comfort for Cassy, and she felt a wave of weakness wash over her as his clasp tightened on hers, and made her concentrate on her steps with almost fanatic fervour in the hope that if she got it right again he would lengthen the distance between them.

'Why don't you just relax?' he said softly, as she made yet another error. 'You're trying too hard.'

This at least was certainly true, and Cassy knew it but could do little about it. 'Perhaps if you gave me a little more room to manoeuvre,' she said breathlessly. 'I was managing all right before, wasn't I?' she added complainingly.

'So you were,' he said with a hint of amusement in his voice, and with a deep sigh released her to her former position. 'Pity, I was enjoying myself,' he teased her with a mocking light in his eyes.

It was too late now to regret her earlier words. She might just as well have said, 'Your nearness is disturbing me,' and be done with it. It was the truth after all, and the worst part about it was that he was well aware of it and found it amusing. In spite of her twenty-two years, she was made to feel very young and very inexperienced, and she didn't think she had disliked anyone as much as she disliked this suave tanned specimen, not even her Uncle George, who in comparison to this man was now appearing in quite a kindly light!

The next dance was a waltz, and Cassy, thinking she had had enough tuition for one night, started to walk towards the perimeter of the dance floor before Justin could claim the dance. She could always say she was tired, couldn't she? she told herself stoutly as she reached the edge of the dance floor, but Justin had other ideas, and she found her hand caught just as she was about to join the watching crowd standing around the floor.

'You'll find this much easier than the quickstep,' he

said breezily, and whirled her into the dance, giving her no chance of refusal.

He's enjoying making me feel uncomfortable, she thought with a sense of disbelief, and wondered if he had become so fond of Sylvia that he was out to punish her for causing Sylvia so much sorrow. It had to be that, there could be no other explanation for his extraordinary behaviour, since she had not missed the fact that each time they swirled round to the beat of the music, he held her closer than was strictly necessary in spite of her earlier request that they should keep their distance.

It looked as if he had meant what he had said about her getting to know him before she left the island, and if this was a taste of what was coming, Cassy wondered if there was a chance of getting an earlier flight back to the U.K.! As much as she had wanted to see the rest of the island, it looked as if it would be far safer if she finished her tour in an armchair by the fireside, reading a travel book from the library!

By the end of the evening, Cassy had learnt how to dance. She had also learnt something else, and that was that she was afraid of Justin Pride. Out of her resentment of his high-handed manner came a fear she had never experienced before, and inexperience was the cause of it. She had tried to act offhand with him, tried to show him in little ways that whatever his opinion was of her, it did not matter one whit to her, but she had failed miserably on all counts, and had to admit defeat.

It wouldn't have mattered quite so much if she had not felt so strongly attracted to him, and hated herself for her weakness, and even if she had had the experi-

ence she knew she lacked in such circumstances, she
had to honestly admit to herself there would be few
women who could have handled the situation, or even
have wanted to.

A few words from Sylvia was all that was needed,
she told herself bitterly, as she took her place beside
Justin in the car at the end of the evening, and felt a
surge of resentment at Sylvia's happy chuckle at something Greg had said. The quietness that prevailed
afterwards told its own story, and Greg appeared to
have lost a little of his shyness in the dark confines of
the back seat.

When they arrived at Cassy's hotel, she knew a
sense of thankfulness and did not linger on her fare-
wells. 'See you tomorrow,' called Sylvia, and Cassy
muttered, 'Not if I can help it,' in a low voice, but
found to her utter frustration that Justin intended to
see her into the hotel.

'Please don't bother,' she said swiftly, feeling panic
rise in her at the thought of him seeing her to her
room and maybe wanting a 'thank you' kiss for his
trouble.

As it turned out, he saw her to the lift, then giving
her a wicked grin, said, 'See you,' as the lift doors
closed between them leaving Cassy, weak with relief,
on her own.

The next morning she slept late, and did not wake
until nine. This was most unusual for her as she was
normally an early riser, and she could only put her
late awakening down to the time change.

Even so, it was a most annoying state of affairs, as
she had promised herself a day on her own, and had
planned to ring Sylvia's hotel early the next morning

and leave a message for her to that effect—early enough for her to be well away on whatever tour she had chosen by the time Sylvia was given the message.

One thing was certain now, and that was that with Greg Storn on the scene Sylvia would not lack company, and the fact that Sylvia was not averse to his attentions gave Cassy no conscience qualms on this score.

She gave an impatient sigh as she emerged from the shower. All she could hope now was that Sylvia had overslept too, and knowing her, Cassy knew this was highly probable; she had never been an early riser in the past.

The phone rang as she was in the middle of dressing, and she gave an exasperated sigh as she picked up the receiver expecting to hear the smooth tones of Justin Pride outlining the treats in store for her that day.

'I'll be over in ten minutes,' said a happy-sounding Sylvia. 'If you haven't had breakfast yet, we'll have it together. I've just waved Greg off, he's playing a match this morning, and Justin's got some business to attend to, so we'll have to amuse ourselves. Anyway, I rather fancy a lazy day, how about you?' she queried.

'That's fine by me,' answered Cassy. Anything was fine by her as long as she could avoid Justin Pride's company.

By the time she was ready to go down to breakfast, Sylvia had arrived, and the two girls took breakfast on the sunlit patio of the hotel.

At the end of the leisurely meal, Sylvia sat back and raised her face to the warm rays of the sun, then looked at the hotel beach in the distance where gay parasols were dotted here and there, and the residents were re-clining in loungers and lapping up the tropical sun-light.

Cassy followed her look. 'I think that's a very good idea, don't you?' she suggested with a twinkle in her eye. 'Might as well see if we can get a tan, too.'

'I was hoping you'd say that,' enthused Sylvia. 'There's plenty of time for us to see the rest of the island, and I do feel lazy,' she gave Cassy a grin. 'I brought swimsuits for us. I was sure you wouldn't have brought that tatty old blue one of yours, and I don't suppose you bothered to buy another one, did you?'

Cassy's eyebrows raised at this. 'Well, I wasn't given much time to think about such mundane items,' she said dryly as the girls made their way back into the hotel to change into their swimsuits.

A short while later they were stretched out on the white sands and letting the heat of the sun seep into their torpid limbs. A large parasol above them pro-tected them from the intensity of the rays as the morn-ing wore on, but the warmth was enough to make them lethargic.

'Poor Cassy,' murmured Sylvia a little drowsily. 'Did Dad give you a bad time?'

Cassy blinked a little, and brought her mind back to the subject Sylvia had raised, although she would much rather have continued watching the small white breakers rolling up to the beach. 'Well, he didn't have it all his own way,' she answered, thinking about the stipulation she had made about the kennels, and realised with a spurt of wonder that she hadn't given the kennels much thought since she had set foot on the island.

'In fact,' she mused, 'I ought to be grateful to you. I would have had a much harder time persuading him to let me have the kennels. As it was, I used this trip as a lever, and it worked.'

Sylvia raised herself on one elbow and looked at Cassy. 'I thought it was all cut and dried,' she said. 'I couldn't see Mrs Peel selling out to anyone else.'

'She might have had to,' replied Cassy musingly. 'There was a time factor involved, you see. She'd found this cottage and was terrified someone else would beat her to it, so she had to have a quick sale, and that meant that I had to approach your father to sell some of my shares in the firm. Not that that worried him, he would buy them up himself, of course, but it did mean I would be moving out and not always available to arrange those dinners he's so fond of giving,' she paused, and gave Sylvia a smile. 'So I'm ashamed to say I used a little blackmail on him. Said I'd come out here and talk to you if he arranged for me to buy the kennels.'

'It wasn't blackmail, Cassy, it was standing up to him,' said Sylvia solemnly. 'It's the only way to make him understand that you mean what you say. That's why I'm sticking it out here, and I can't think of a nicer place to make a stand, can you?' she asked with a hint of humour in her voice.

Cassy lay back and stretched out her legs in an utterly relaxed action before she answered a little plaintively, 'No, I'm in perfect accord with you there. My only complaint is the way you selected me for the villainous role in your highly imaginative farce.'

Sylvia let out a low chuckle. 'I thought it was quite good myself,' she said, without a trace of apology. 'It didn't put Justin off, though, did it? I noticed you were getting quite chummy during the dancing.'

Cassy sat bolt upright at this and stared at Sylvia. 'Correction,' she snapped, 'he was trying to get chummy with me. There is a difference, you know. And while we're about it, don't include me in any further tours with him. I can't stand the man!' she added crossly.

'Methinks the lady doth protest too much,' misquoted Sylvia with a wide mischievous grin, and gave a moue of mock sorrow. 'Poor Justin! I had a feeling he was quite interested in you.'

'Of course he is!' Cassy retorted smartly, 'only because he's sorry for you. He has a dig at me every chance he gets—and it's not as if it's any of his business—and I told him so!' she added heatedly. 'So if you really want me to enjoy what's left of my holiday, count me out of any further plans he might come up with.'

'Oh, dear,' said Sylvia softly, 'he did get your goat, didn't he?' She gave a loud sigh. 'Perhaps it wasn't such a good idea after all, and I was sure everything was going to be all right,' she added wistfully, then shot Cassy a look from under her long blonde lashes. 'I don't know what excuse I'm going to make for you,' she said worriedly. 'It's not going to be easy fooling him.'

Cassy's lips folded obstinately at this. 'You surprise me,' she answered curtly, 'I thought it was incredibly easy to fool him. Tell him we've had another row; tell him I'm absolutely determined to continue my pursuit of the golden goal—tell him anything—I just don't want another day in his company!'

Sylvia's eyes widened as she stared back at the vehement Cassy, then she looked swiftly away again and swallowed. 'I'll tell him the truth,' she said quietly. 'I ought to have owned up when you arrived.'

For a second Cassy was tempted to accept Sylvia's belated attempt to put things right, but at a vision of the furious Justin reading the riot act to Sylvia, and offering his apologies to herself, she almost shuddered. Sylvia did not know that it was really fear of the man that had made Cassy react in this totally unnatural manner. Had it been anyone else but Justin Pride, she would have shrugged the whole episode off, and perhaps even seen the funny side of it, but her sense of humour did not stretch that far, particularly when the man concerned had such a spellbinding effect on her.

'Oh no, you don't!' Cassy got out breathlessly. 'Don't you dare own up now. It's much too late, don't you see that?' She caught Sylvia's hand. 'Look, dear, I'm not really blaming you for what happened,' she sighed. 'In a way I blame myself for not realising just how unhappy you were. If I hadn't been so caught up with my own affairs this wouldn't have happened.' She squeezed her hand. 'I'm as much to blame as you are. It's just that that man gets me on the raw. I can't explain it; he's too smooth, and too ...' she searched for the right word.

'Too kind?' finished Sylvia with one eyebrow raised and a certain knowing look in her eyes.

'That wasn't the word I was looking for,' replied Cassy ironically. ' "Sophisticated" is more apt, don't you think? Anyway,' she went on quickly, 'I'm determined to keep out of his way from now on, and I'm relying on you to help me to do this.'

'But that means that I won't see much of you while you're here,' complained Sylvia mutinously.

Cassy shrugged lightly. 'Well, you can't have it both ways, and I want your promise that you'll leave things as they are, and not complicate the issue by making any more confessions, true or untrue. Agreed?' she asked the crestfallen Sylvia, who gave a miserable nod of agreement. 'Good!' went on Cassy feeling as if a load had been taken off her. 'And cheer up! There's bound to be days when our mutual friend is otherwise occupied, like this morning, and we can always get together again—just give me a ring so that I can keep the morning or the afternoon free. Not,' she added meaningly, 'that I imagine that you'll have that much free time, going by the way a certain young man was looking at you last night!'

At the mention of Greg, Sylvia immediately brightened. 'He's nice, isn't he, Cassy?' she said enthusiastically, 'and I did so want a date with him. I'd seen him often, just had a chat now and again, but you saw how shy he was. I was sure he wanted to ask me out but couldn't work up enough courage. I think he asked Justin to fix it for him.' She was silent for a few seconds as her eyes scanned the sea shore. 'It's absolutely ridiculous, I know, but it's as if we were meant to meet. I know him so well, yet hardly at all. It's as if we were right for each other, and I somehow know we belong.'

She gave Cassy a sideways grin. 'Oh, I know I've had crushes on other men, particularly handsome ones, but they were only crushes, I can see that now. This is real, and this is for ever. I know it,' she said simply.

Cassy gave her a startled look. She didn't want Sylvia to get hurt. 'It's probably the island,' she said dryly, trying to make light of her words. 'I've heard tropical islands do things to you. Just keep one foot on the ground, dear, that way it's not so far to fall.'

To Cassy's further consternation, Sylvia made no attempt to assure her of the sincerity of her words, but just said quietly, 'You'll see,' and left it at that.

CHAPTER FIVE

CASSY and Sylvia parted company just after four, as Sylvia had arranged to meet Greg at five. 'I only hope Justin hasn't made any plans for the evening,' she said a little worriedly before she left, but Cassy remained firm and ignored the silent plea.

'Just say you've a solo date with Greg,' she said complacently, 'and that I've made other plans. It should be easy.' She gave the worried Sylvia a smile. 'Don't worry, dear. I've a feeling he'll be relieved that all is taken care of. He must have some other things he'd rather be doing than act as nursemaid to a couple of little green girls!'

This ought to have reassured Sylvia, but judging by her hopeful nod she was not utterly convinced of this, but had to abide by Cassy's decision to bow out of any future tours.

As the bedroom door closed behind her, Cassy felt relief flow over her. Greg would see that she was kept fully occupied, and that left Cassy free to follow her own inclinations for the rest of her holiday.

Her step was light as she walked over to the dressing table and retrieved the itinerary she had carefully mapped out earlier, and studied the brochures. There were several evening tours listed, but they consisted of visits to the island's night spots, and Cassy felt no inclination towards any such entertainment, and even if she had, the chances were that she would run into

Sylvia or Greg, or worse still, Justin Pride!

With a sigh of contentment she put a tick against one of the listed tours. She would take that one the next day, and have dinner in the hotel this evening, and an early night. It was a wonderful feeling to be able to plan one's own entertainment and not feel beholden to anyone else. She thanked providence for the timely intervention of Greg Storn, as she had no worries now about letting Sylvia down, and she could just please herself. All she had to remember to do was to book the tour before she retired for the night.

The sun was still shining with almost as much strength as it had earlier in the day as she went back to the beach to continue her sunbathing. She noted that further along the beach there were several tables set out under large parasols from where refreshments were being served, and hoping that it would be possible to obtain a cup of tea, she made her way through the re-clining sunbathers strewn out on the white sands, and towards the refreshment area.

The tea was not quite the same as that served at home—for instance, tea bags were used, and instead of asking for 'milk' one had to request 'cream', but once all this was straightened out, the beverage was quite acceptable.

After her thirst had been quenched, Cassy settled down on one of the numerous loungers and watched a few yachts tacking round a buoy in the distance, the bright red and orange and blue sails adding even more colour to the naturally bright vista.

While she watched the different tactics employed in what she presumed to be a race of some kind, her thoughts returned to Sylvia and Greg, and the surprising statement Sylvia had made earlier. She had seemed so positive, thought Cassy, and for all her 'mad moments' she was normally a basically sensible person. She had never minded being teased, and was always ready to admit her mistakes, and in a way, very much like Cassy herself. She also had the same sense of humour as Cassy, yet she had not risen to Cassy's teasing comment on 'tropical effects'.

Cassy turned over on to her stomach to let the sun caress her back. Sylvia's reaction had been much like her own, she mused, when Sylvia had teased her about Justin Pride. She moved restlessly and readjusted her position on the lounger; she did not want to think about that man, or the effect he had on her—and that was tropical, there was not much doubt of that, and at least she had had the sense to see it.

One thing was certain now, she thought sadly, if the romance Sylvia was so sure would blossom happened to fizzle out, then she would be heading home like a homing pigeon, for there was no doubt that it would hit her hard if her hopes came to nothing and Greg was only indulging in a holiday romance.

Cassy's smooth forehead creased at the thought; from what she had seen of him she felt this was most unlikely. As Sylvia had said, one had a feeling about such things, and Cassy had to admit that in all probability it was the real thing for both of them.

It had not been hard to elicit a few facts from Sylvia about Greg. He was a professional golfer, and was apparently quite well known in the States. He had, confided Sylvia, been very reticent about his previous wins, and she had taken this as a sign that he had done very well in his chosen career. Cassy had also learnt that he came of a golfing family, and he was now upholding the family tradition of making their mark in the golfing world.

At least the family was respectable, Cassy thought with an inward grin as she visualised her uncle's reaction to the news of his daughter's involvement with Greg—if it ever got that far, she reminded herself. She gave another small smile as she recalled his remarks about the possibility of her picking up 'some beachcomber'. If anyone had been landed with a 'beachcomber' she had! A very high class one, of course, but definitely a soldier of fortune with no visible means of support.

Her smile faded on this thought. She was not being exactly fair to Justin in labelling him as such, she didn't know enough about him to categorically label him as a playboy. She gave a small sigh. She couldn't see what else he could be, living as he did. He would know all the best families, and with his looks and charm would have the entrée to wherever the moneyed set settled, hence his habit, as she had learned from Sylvia, of travelling round the islands.

Her lovely blue eyes narrowed at this thought; he would always be sure of a welcome—particularly from the rich lonely women who required an escort. Cassy found this thought not only distasteful but hurtful, and she was vaguely surprised at the intensity of her feelings. What did it matter to her what he did, who he saw, or where he went? It was his way of life and nothing to do with her.

She lay back and closed her eyes in an effort to shut out a few unwelcome thoughts that were hovering at the back of her mind. The kennels—she would concentrate on them, and how she would furnish the house when she got back. There was so much ahead of her, so why waste time thinking about someone who could never mean anything to her once she had left the island, and whose existence she would have completely forgotten by the time the plane touched down in England.

After a few determined attempts to concentrate on what would be essential items to be purchased as soon as she returned home, Cassy gave it up, finding it impossible to give the matter serious thought. It all seemed so far away and somehow improbable, and considering it was all that she had ever wanted, she found this state of affairs most disquieting, and blamed the island for her lack of interest.

As she prepared herself for her lonely dinner in the hotel, she hoped she would be lucky in obtaining a solitary table as she did not feel in the mood for breezy conversation. She was not a good mixer, and found it hard to keep up a sparkling contribution on whatever subject was introduced.

She had not been too sure of what to wear, either, and had settled for a maroon three-quarter-length tiered skirt with a peasant styled blouse. That was quite passable, she thought, as she gave herself a last look over before going to face the first sitting.

An abrupt knock on her bedroom door made her firm her lips together as she waited for Sylvia to enter, and if she was hoping to persuade Cassy to join them for the evening, she had a disappointment coming! Her brows lifted slightly when the knock was repeated, this time with more insistence, and she realised it was not Sylvia, and felt a little calmer as she went to answer the knock. It was probably one of the hotel staff, she thought, and a second later she was staring into Justin's grey mocking eyes.

Her first shocked reaction was to step back and close the door smartly, but she managed to control this purely defensive action since it was hardly polite.

'Good!' said Justin, giving her a swift appraisal. 'I do like punctuality.'

Cassy continued to stare at him, then swallowed hastily as the old resentment of the man overcame her. 'I was not aware we had a date,' she said coldly. 'I was just going down to dinner.'

He just looked at her, and she felt the colour rise in her cheeks. Then he gave an elaborate sigh. 'I've already had to cancel a table for four,' he said slowly but meaningly, 'and have no intention of cancelling my amended order for a table for two. I can understand Sylvia and Greg's wish for a solo date, what's your excuse?' he demanded.

Cassy wished fervently that she could tell him. 'Sylvia told me of her plans for this evening,' she lied, 'so naturally I thought ...' She hesitated, then as her eyes met his very knowing ones, she saw no reason to beat about the bush. 'Surely there's something else you'd rather be doing, isn't there?' she demanded. 'We're very grateful for the trouble you've gone to on our behalf so far, but really there's no need to put yourself out of your routine like this.' Her blue eyes met his squarely as she said, 'I'm sure you can find someone else to take out to dinner, even at this short notice.'

Justin continued to watch her, and Cassy almost squirmed under his direct scrutiny. She had spoken the truth after all, and he should be grateful to her!

'As a matter of fact, I suppose I could,' he answered casually, and Cassy knew he was not boasting, just stating a plain fact, 'but I'm not,' he said bluntly. 'I happen to want to take you out to dinner.'

Cassy's cheeks tinged a deeper pink. 'Why?' she demanded with a glint in her eyes. If he could be blunt, so could she!

'I think the answer would surprise you,' he said softly, and gave her a challenging look. 'Well? Are you ready?'

A confused Cassy just looked at him; he was railroading her again into doing something she did not want to do. 'Is this the way you usually make dates?' she asked with a touch of incredulity in her voice.

Justin gave a low chuckle, and taking the key she held in her hand from her, shepherded her out of the room and into the corridor, then locked the door for her before replying breezily, 'Only when necessary.'

The restaurant Justin took her to was Spanish in every conceivable way. Food and decor echoed the past grandeur of Spain, and as they walked into the dining room, the rich colours of burnt orange and gold painted on the walls and ceiling that glowed in the ornate lighting gave the large room an intimate atmosphere that was not lost on Cassy.

This time Justin did not hand her the menu but ordered the meal in his usual autocratic way, and Cassy, trying not to look as overawed as she felt, gazed around at what looked at first sight a very small restaurant, but appearances were deceptive, for she noticed that at the end of the room was an alcove that led to further dining space. Her attention was next held by the various objets d'art hung on the walls around the room, that consisted mostly of plaques with carved effigies depicting bygone battle scenes of proud armour-clad Spaniards with swords upraised, putting their enemies to flight.

So absorbed did Cassy become in these detailed plaques that she was not aware that she was receiving just as much scrutiny from the silent man who sat opposite her, and it wasn't until she switched her attention from one plaque to another that she became aware of it, and glanced back at him, flushing a little under that steady gaze of his.

'Why are you called Cassy?' he asked. 'I presume your name is Cassandra?'

Cassy gave a nod of confirmation, and still feeling embarrassed, she tried to bring a light note into the conversation. 'You must agree it's rather a mouthful,' she said lightly. 'No one calls me Cassandra now. My father used to, but as it was his choice of name, I suppose he would.' She was silent after this, not knowing what else to say.

'And you lost your parents when you were quite young?' he asked.

Again Cassy nodded, well aware of what was going through his mind, and at any moment now he would start to question her about her supposed affair with Sylvia's father. He would have no conscience about bringing up such a personal subject, but Cassy had no intention of discussing such an embarrassing situation with him—then or ever! 'What a quaint place this is,' she said quickly, and stared round at the room again. 'Are those plaques made of oak? They look as though they might be,' she went on, now almost babbling in her anxiety to keep the conversation on purely impersonal lines.

Justin gave her a long considering look that told her that he knew very well that she was determined to evade the issue, and he was just as determined to pursue it. However, he answered her query casually enough. 'Very probably; I imagine they're extremely weighty objects.'

The waiter appeared with the first course, much to Cassy's relief, and the subject she was so keen to drop was put aside for the time being, although something told her she would not be able to avoid the issue for long, particularly as she did not know how they were going to fill in the rest of the evening. As far as she could see, this was purely a restaurant with no facilities for dancing, and that meant every chance of a cosy chit-chat later with the very knowing character sitting opposite her. Cassy wondered which was the worst of the two evils, that, or spending the evening in his arms on the dance floor. Either way, it was not a very bright outlook for her, and as Mrs Peel was wont to say when things were not going exactly smoothly, 'Everything points to misery!'

After the meal, that was surprisingly good in spite of the fact that the dishes were entirely new to her palate, and were wholly Spanish, Cassy sat back feeling replete, but rather apprehensive as to the next move on the agenda, and did not know whether to be worried or relieved when he suggested they take in a night show. At least he made it sound like a suggestion, but Cassy, who was beginning to know him a little better, knew that that was just what they would do. Justin had already made his plans for the evening, and all she was expected to do was to go along in his autocratic wake.

As the show had begun by the time they reached the chosen night club, Cassy found herself being guided to a table in semi-darkness with Justin's arm around her slim waist, and she felt that a slight touch on her arm would have been enough of a guide for her, without the closer proximity he was giving her, but the feminine side of her had no objection!

A short while later, in spite of her certainty that it would be impossible for her to enjoy herself in his company, she soon became enthralled by the exciting and seemingly impossible feats performed by the entertainers, particularly the limbo dancers, as she watched their tall lithe bodies slither under a raised cane less than a foot above ground, with a gracefulness that had to be seen to be believed.

This was followed by other acts; there was a fire dancer, and a shake dancer who in Caribbean fashion danced to calypso music, and finally the foot-tapping rhythm of the steel dums.

When the show ended and Justin escorted Cassy back to the car, she had to admit to herself that she had thoroughly enjoyed the evening, and in all fairness she had to tell him so. This she would do when she bade him goodnight, also thank him for the trouble he had gone to to provide an evening's entertainment for her.

Her thoughts roamed on as the car started up and glided out of the car parking area. He had behaved so correctly during the evening that her previous fears of his demanding some compensation for his company had now entirely vanished, since she was now convinced that he was putting himself out on Sylvia's behalf. Although this meant that the subject that she had successfully avoided so far would soon be brought into sharp focus again, Cassy was so lulled by the excellent dinner and wine, and the following entertainment, that she felt no animosity towards him; how could she, when he was rooting for Sylvia's happiness?

In this complacent, almost lethargic, but pleasantly so, mood, Cassy wanted to tell him the truth, the whole truth, and nothing but the truth. She gave a little chuckle as these thoughts went through her mind. It was as if she was in the witness box fighting for her good name—which in a manner of speaking was precisely what she was trying to do.

Her chuckle brought Justin's look swivelling round at her before he gave the road his attention again. 'Happy?' he queried lightly.

Cassy stole a quick look at his strong profile before she answered softly, 'I thoroughly enjoyed the evening. Thank you, Mr Pride. I really do appreciate your giving up your time like this.'

Justin gave her another of those swift appraisals of his, then replied in a slightly aggrieved tone, 'I would prefer you to call me Justin. Mr Pride sounds so formal, doesn't it? I'm glad you enjoyed the evening. Tomorrow we'll take in the rest of the island. I'm not sure about Sylvia, though; I've a feeling she'll want to watch Greg's game; it's a semi-final, you know.'

Cassy blinked hastily and tried to arouse some of the resentment she had felt before at the way he took so much for granted where she was concerned. Whether it was due to the wine or not, she only knew a sense of wellbeing, and more than that—an inner glow of happiness that they would be together again the following day. Even if it was the wine that had mellowed her outlook, she really did not care, she felt so happy and warm inside—and wanted.

She swallowed on this last thought; she had known what it felt like to be wanted purely for her expertise in arranging dinners, hence her uncle's bid to keep her in the household. But this was a different kind of feeling, and her whole being glowed when she recalled the way Justin had said that he had wanted to take her out to dinner.

She was so immersed in her thoughts that she did not notice that they had not gone back to the hotel but had moved away from the city, and the car was now steadily climbing up a winding coastal road.

Cassy sat up straight as the knowledge hit her, and all her previous fears returned leaving her feeling cheated and very let down. Where was he taking her? What did she know of this man, anyway? And come to that, what did Sylvia know of him? She swallowed. He was just an aquaintance she had made in the hotel who appeared to be a charming, helpful man—but was he? She gulped quickly—it appeared she was on the point of finding out—and felt extremely frightened.

Whatever happened, she told herself, trying to calm her heartbeats that were beating a staccato not unlike the music she had been enjoying a short while before, she had to stay in the car. She would be safer that way, she told herself as they glided to a halt on a kind of plateau.

When Justin suggested they get out and admire the view, she hoped she did not sound as frightened as she felt as she feigned a yawn and said she would rather stay where she was, and yes, it was a wonderful view, but could they get back to the hotel, for she really was tired and had meant to have an early night that night.

'It won't take a minute,' he said mildly. 'I promise to take you back directly. You can't possibly see as much from the car seat. Come on,' and he gently pulled her out of her seat.

If Justin had been a known murderer, Cassy would still have found herself holding his hand and walking to the edge of the plateau. Such was his strange magnetic hold over her, and she weakly told herself that she had tried, hadn't she?

Even in her slightly stupefied state, she was able to appreciate the magnificent view from the plateau that looked over a bay that was full of twinkling lights, and these, she assumed, would be the various craft at anchor in the bay.

From her position she could now see that there were several cars drawn up a little further away from them, ostensibly to admire the view, but were probably lovers, and this thought made her feel immensely sad, too sad to even make up for the relief she felt when she realised that they were not alone. She now felt foolish, and very mean in condemning what had turned out to be yet another thoughtful action on Justin's behalf.

'It's wonderful,' she said softly, as her eyes skimmed the brilliant sky whose stars seemed enormous and somehow closer than the ones at home. If he wanted to kiss her, she told herself, she would make no demur, in fact she rather hoped he did, it was the least she could do after her misjudgment of him.

To her chagrin, however, he made no such demand on her and, slightly put out, Cassy gave a quick nod when he asked, 'Ready?' and followed him back to the car.

On the journey back to the hotel, Cassy spent most of the time wondering if he had noticed her earlier turmoil, and worse still, the thoughts that had gone through her mind. It was all she could do not to tell him to stop the car and have everything out with him before they reached her hotel, where he would, no doubt, politely escort her to the lift as before, and after telling her what time he would pick her up the following morning, wish her good night.

Her heart skipped a beat on the thought that he might decide to back out of the previous arrangement, and she conceded miserably that she really couldn't blame him if he did.

They reached the hotel, and as presumed by Cassy, Justin stood beside her while they waited for the lift. 'Nine-thirty too early for you?' he asked casually.

The relief Cassy felt far outweighed her earlier disappointment in his exemplary behaviour on the plateau, and she didn't know it, but her happiness glowed in her lovely eyes as she answered breathlessly, 'Of course not. I'll be ready.'

Justin's eyes narrowed slightly as he took in her slight flush, and he gave a satisfied nod, then gave her a slow heart-stopping smile, and there was almost a caress in his, 'See you,' as the lift doors opened and Cassy had to leave him.

The way she felt, it was a wonder she was able to recall what floor to ask for when the question was put to her by the smiling lift attendant, but she answered in a dazed way and sank back into her dreams again, coming out of them for a short space of time when her floor was reached, and the slightly amused attendant had to repeat the number twice before she realised it was her floor. With a feeling that she was walking on air, she drifted out of the lift and down the corridor to her room.

Cassy was irrevocably in love, but she didn't know it. She only knew that she was exceedingly happy, and after what seemed a disastrous start to the holiday she had been forced to take, she was now going to enjoy herself for the first time for years. Sylvia was happy too, she told herself. She too had found someone to enjoy her holiday with, and everything was wonderful!

Apart from these thoughts, Cassy did not probe further, and would have been surprised if someone had told her the real cause of her jubilation, and she would have instantly rejected the mere idea that she had fallen in love with Justin Pride.

The following morning she prepared herself for the day out with Justin in an aura of happy expectation, and wouldn't allow any other thoughts to intrude on her happiness. She wouldn't be here for all that long, so she might as well enjoy herself while she could. All too soon she would be back home, working out where to put the annual overflow of animals, and seriously thinking of enlarging the whole site. There was ample room for this, she knew, but Mrs Peel had never got down to it, and had been content to just manage for the extra month or so while the holiday rush was on.

Those thoughts occupied her mind while she took her time over her toilet, making sure that she looked her best, but with her glowing eyes and soft peach-tinted complexion, she would have looked good in whatever she wore, such was the difference love made.

Her soft pink sleeveless dress with flared skirt suited the occasion, she thought, as she gave herself a critical last-minute look in the mirror before going down to await Justin's arrival, allowing herself a good five minutes before the appointed time so that she would be ready and waiting when he made his appearance.

CHAPTER SIX

THERE was a lot of activity in the hotel reception area as Cassy sat down in one of the chairs to await Justin's arrival. While she waited, she amused herself watching the guests gathering in various groups according to what tour they were taking, and smiled as a harassed-looking mother ordered her son stay by her side and not wander away as they would be leaving for the tour any moment now.

The arrival of the tour operators caused more flurry, and the lists were checked to ascertain that everyone was present. However, on one of the tours there appeared to be one person missing, a Miss someone or other, and Cassy, sitting quietly on her own taking all the activity in, felt herself come under a hard stare from the operator who was one short, and she shook her head at him, smilingly answering the unspoken question. He would have to direct his enquiries elsewhere if he wanted to track down his missing client.

A glance at her watch told her it was just past the half hour, and she directed her attention to the entrance to the hotel. At any moment now Justin should be arriving, she told herself happily.

When there was no sign of him a quarter of an hour later, Cassy began to wonder what the hold-up was, and when her name was paged she got up to answer the summons with a feeling of relief. He was going to be late, something had held him up, but it didn't matter, she told herself as she picked up the telephone from the booth the receptionist had indicated; she would be here, she would wait all morning if necessary.

'Cassy?' Sylvia's voice came floating down the line to her, giving her a slight shock followed by an instant worry that something had happened to Justin. 'I ought to have rung you before, but you know I'm a late riser,' she went on, and Cassy wanted to shout out at her the burning question in her mind. 'Justin left a message for me to ring you before nine-thirty, to say he couldn't make it today. Something's turned up and he's had to go over to one of the out islands, but he hopes to be back in time to take you to dinner. I'm sorry, dear, I felt awful when I found this message waiting—still,' she went on, now sounding a little amused, 'I don't suppose the news will cause you any heartache, do you? More in the nature of a let-off, I'd say. How do you fancy watching a game of golf?' she ended gaily.

Cassy managed to answer in what she hoped sounded her natural voice, yet disappointment was flowing through her, clouding all else from her mind. 'No, thank you, dear,' she said, 'I'd be bored stiff. You go ahead. I hope Greg wins; Justin told me it was an important game.'

'It's a semi-final,' replied Sylvia proudly, 'and I've a feeling he'll get through. But what will you do?' she asked solicitously.

'Oh, I'll be okay,' replied Cassy with more brightness than she felt. 'I'll have another lazy day on the beach. I haven't got as long as you have to get myself a tan, have I?' she asked dryly.

'Are you sure?' queried Sylvia, then went on to add, 'Well, at least you'll have company tonight. I expect

Justin will turn up. I only wish you liked him a bit more. He does like you, Cassy.'

Cassy swallowed a lump in her throat. It looked like it, didn't it? The only full day he had arranged for them to have, and he had cancelled it to go traipsing about wherever it was that Sylvia had mentioned. She forced herself to give a hard chuckle. 'I think it's mutual. He's only waiting to give me another lecture on your behalf. I think I'm going to be very busy this evening,' she hinted caustically, 'so would you leave him a message to that effect?' she asked. 'Tell him not to bother to make any arrangements for dinner. I'm sure he'll be tired anyway. I shall take one of the evening tours. I haven't made up my mind which yet, but one or two look interesting,' she lied stoutly.

'Poor Justin,' said Sylvia softly. 'I'm not convinced about his intentions where you're concerned, and you could be wrong, you know. Well, just give me a ring or leave a message at the desk if you get tired of your own company. See you,' and she rang off leaving a miserable Cassy to replace her receiver.

And to think, she fumed as she headed back to her room, she could have taken the place of that missing tourist who was probably sleeping late and had not bothered to inform the desk that she would not be taking the morning tour. As for Sylvia—— Why hadn't the wretched man phoned her himself? He must have left extremely early, too early to be able to contact her. She supposed that was the answer—had to be—but even so, he could have left a message at her hotel, couldn't he, and she wouldn't have had to sit like a zombie in the reception waiting for someone who wasn't going to turn up!

In all honesty she had the answer to that one, too. Justin had wanted Sylvia to know that Cassy would be alone all that day, and would probably make arrangements to include her in whatever she and Greg had planned to do after the match.

A twinge of conscience on his part? she wondered, as she got into the lift and gave her floor number to the waiting attendant. Well, he needn't worry about her, she hadn't wanted his company in the first place, had she? She bit her lower lip as the memory of the look he had given her as he had said, 'See you,' when she got into this selfsame lift last night. Not if I see you first! she vowed to herself fervently.

The lift attendant, taking due note of her bleak expression, wisely did not comment on what a fine day it was, but kept his eyes fixed on the floor numbers. He'd seen it all before—one minute they were walking on air, the next down in the dumps, for he had been on duty the previous evening and had practically had to push this pretty girl out of the lift when her floor had been reached, so absorbed had she been in her world of dreams.

Old Sam Brown sighed inwardly. There wasn't much he didn't know about folks, he had been doing the job for the past thirty years, and it was surprising how much you noticed, if you had eyes to see, of the glimpses of other folks' worlds, even in his restricted working area. That man who had seen the girl off last night—well, he knew him, in fact there wouldn't be many of the island's regular visitors that he didn't know. And if this pretty young thing had hopes there, he'd advise her to forget them. There were plenty of others looking in the same direction, but that man was nobody's fool, he'd had plenty of practice in avoiding the strategically laid nets to ensnare him in the past, he couldn't see this young innocent miss pulling off the coup of the year, which it would be, he ruminated slowly, if such a thing happened.

Completely unaware of the thoughts going through the silent attendant's head, Cassy stepped out of the lift and made her way to her room, blissfully ignorant of the way his sad old eyes followed her stiff erect figure, and the good wishes he sent in her direction for a speedy recovery from her malady.

Once the door was closed behind her, Cassy's eyes brimmed over with unspilt tears, and she brushed them away impatiently. What a fool she was! and what a wonderful let-off she had just been given. She ought to be rejoicing, there was nothing like the slap of a wet towel in the face to bring one to one's senses, and Justin's let-down had made her feel just like that. When she thought of her earlier feelings she felt her cheeks burn with shame. She had acted just like a teenager on a first crush, throwing sense and even propriety to the winds. Look how she had wanted him to kiss her on the plateau last night—and how frustrated she had felt when he had shown no sign of even wanting to!

It wasn't a bit like her to act like that. In the past she had had no time for stolen kisses, or the giggling half-surrender tactics employed by other girls of her age. To her way of thinking, it had all been a stupid way of going on, and she had much better things to do with her time, such as helping to scrub out kennels ready for new occupants.

A nasty thought then struck her. Was she making up

for lost time now? And had she chosen Justin Pride to be the recipient of her affections? She gulped hastily —if so, she had had more of a let-off than she knew! Fate had smiled kindly on her before she made an all-time fool of herself, it seemed.

Her small chin stuck out defiantly. Well, she would accept the timely warning, she told herself firmly, for there was no doubt that the man was extremely attractive. There was also no doubt that she had no control over her emotions where he was concerned. He made her feel just like a lump of plasticine ready to be moulded into whatever shape he wished to mould her.

Her hands clenched into small fists on this thought. No one, but no one, would mould her into anything else but what she wanted to be! She was Cassy Aden, and master of her ship, and would always be. She had a bright, interesting future ahead of her, and was not likely to throw all that away on the whims of one man, simply because she found him devastatingly attractive. She might be inexperienced, but she could see a come-on when it was handed out to her—and that was just what that look of his had been when he had left her last night.

She sat down wearily on the bed; all because he felt sorry for Sylvia. If she hadn't been as level-headed as she was, she would have fallen hook, line and sinker for his tactics in removing her interest—or so-called interest—from Sylvia's father to him—whereupon, she thought grimly, he would have dropped her like a hot brick and not had a mite of conscience about it. In his view she deserved all she got, for she hadn't forgotten the way he had said, 'Is it going to be worth it?' and

something about hurting Sylvia. Oh no, he would have
no compunction whatsoever.

Her eyes fell upon her hands now twisted together.
Was this why he had arranged to meet her the following day after giving her the full treatment of his fatal
charm, then cancelling the date at the last moment?
Her soft lips twisted; of course it was! He had known
only too well of her feelings on the plateau; that he
had only to reach for her and she would have melted in
his arms. She drew in a ragged breath. It was cruel,
but very effective. He would put in an appearance for
dinner, he had got it all worked out, and it would not
be the first time he had employed such tactics, she presumed shrewdly, by which time she was supposed to be
so grateful for his charming company that she would
have been like butter in his hand.

At least, she told herself ironically, she was one step
ahead of him. His plan had not worked, not on her
anyway, but had had the reverse effect and had brought
her to her senses. To think she had almost told him the
truth last night! Actually longed to tell him—and had
felt ashamed for the way Sylvia had hoodwinked him!
Although there was a little more to it than that, she
had to admit to herself honestly. She had wanted him
to know that she was entirely innocent of the charge
laid against her—and why? Because she had been
fool enough to let her feelings get the better of her
normally sensible outlook.

Her hands clenched the cover on the bed. She had
ten more days to go, and somehow she had to steer
well clear of that man! She would take all the tours
going if necessary, evening ones as well! It no longer
bothered her that the evening tours would consist of

visits to night clubs. Even if she did run into Justin
Pride at one of them, she would be with a group, and
would have a good excuse for avoiding his company.

With an urgency that was totally uncalled for, seeing
that Justin was not even on the island, Cassy grabbed
her brochures, and not even waiting for the lift, ran
down the stairs to reception and spent the next quarter
of an hour booking tours with the resident tour operators, and not until she had all the necessary tickets
in her hand, and the times of assembly written down,
did she feel utterly relaxed and able to look forward
to the rest of the day.

Back in her room, Cassy changed into the swimming
costume that Sylvia had left for her use, then slipping
on a blouse and skirt, and collecting a towel and her
sun lotion, she was ready for a morning on the beach
with the comforting thought that from now on her
time was fully booked, and she would not be available
for any other plans Justin Pride might or might not
have in mind.

She was so pleased with herself that she hummed a
little tune while she waited for the lift, and old Sam's
eyebrows rose as he noted the sudden change of mood
in his now happy passenger, and gave it entirely the
wrong interpretation!

After lunch, Cassy got ready for the first of the
afternoon tours, and dressed in a light trouser suit of
a deep tan colour, with a peach blouse that suited her
chestnut colouring, she was ready to enjoy the tour and
went down to the given assembly point.

There had been three tours to choose from, and as
Cassy had seen a little of the town she had chosen one
of the island tours. When all the names had been ticked

off on the list, the guide assigned to them for the afternoon, shepherded his flock into the waiting mini-buses, and as Cassy took her place in the bus, some of her earlier enthusiasm was dampened by a sharp feeling of loneliness as she listened to the other guests hailing one another as they spotted friends who had settled for the same tour, and wished that Sylvia had been with her.

This depression, however, did not last for long, particularly when she reminded herself of the only other alternative; she could have gone along with Sylvia and Greg, but had chosen not to—or she could have sunbathed all day and waited for Justin to collect her for dinner, but she had chosen not to—so what was she complaining about? she upbraided herself sternly. She *would* enjoy herself! and if things got really bad, she could always catch an earlier flight home.

This thought reminded her that she really ought to write to her uncle and tell him that she had contacted Sylvia and that she hoped to be able to persuade her to come back with her. Her lovely eyes narrowed on this thought; it wasn't strictly the truth, but it would allay any further action on his part until she had had a chance to put him into the picture. She nodded her head. Yes, she would do that as soon as she got back to the hotel. She would also tell him that she had decided to stay for a fortnight, and make the most of her holiday. The extra week would give her time to size up the situation between Sylvia and Greg, and if it was really serious, it was up to Sylvia to put him into the picture.

'On your left is the Governor's residence,' said the

tour guide, bringing Cassy's musings to an abrupt end, and directing her attention to a large white imposing-looking building set on a terraced slope, and reached by a series of stone steps behind the high ornamental gates guarding the entrance.

From then on Cassy concentrated on the tour. She saw a small Chinese village with small pagoda-style villas, and learnt that one could book a holiday there should the fancy take one. The pagodas set among the island's luxuriant foliage made it a pleasant prospect, for the village was set high on a hill and away from the noise and bustle of the town.

As the bus passed along narrow roads, Cassy gazed with fascination at the thick vegetation on either side of her, and on one occasion found she need only put her hand out of the window and she could actually touch a clump of bananas growing in a nursery garden. The tropical fruit trees were pointed out to them as they passed them, and names were reeled off, names of numerous exotic fruit only hitherto found in frozen packets at the larger supermarkets at home.

The various residences they passed were mainly bungalows, with plenty of ground attached that inevitably grew the island's flowering trees, the most prominent being the double flowering poinsettia with its bright red blossoms. On passing one rather large residence, Cassy saw a notice on the gate that stated 'Bad dog', and smiled at the thought that it was obviously a warning to would-be burglars, and would be understood as such by the islanders.

So the day wore on; it was interesting, yet in her heart Cassy knew she would have enjoyed it all so much more if a certain person had happened to be with her. Sylvia's presence, she tried to convince herself, would have made all the difference, but it was not Sylvia she missed, but a tall, tanned, handsome man.

The time of assembly for the night club visit that evening was given as eight o'clock, and Cassy, taking no chances of Justin tracking her down before the start of the tour, made an early start of getting ready, and as soon as she had changed into her one and only long skirt, and the same peasant blouse she had worn the previous evening, went down and settled in one of the hotel's numerous lounges until it was time to put in an appearance for the tour. She deliberately chose the most crowded lounge, and sitting in a very convenient chair directly behind a large sprawling flower arrangement, she defied anyone to spot her position, even the eagle-eyed Justin Pride!

When the time had come for her to make her appearance, she went to join the small crowd now assembled outside the hotel, but her step slightly faltered as she noted with some consternation that the waiting tourists seemed to be already paired off, and only the thought of Justin kept her going forward.

When they were all assembled Cassy found to her great relief that she was not the only unattached person in the group, since there were two other women; one an elderly spinster who looked slightly out of place against the rest of the party, and made Cassy wonder if she had somehow got booked on the wrong tour. The other was a girl of Cassy's age, a pretty, petite, blue-eyed blonde, who didn't really look as if she was enjoying herself. The reason for this was soon made clear to Cassy, as she heard the girl refer to the spinster as 'Aunt Mary', and there was no doubt that 'Aunt Mary' was there purely to keep a strict eye on her niece, and that meant that the girl was probably younger than Cassy had at first thought her.

There was also one unattached male in the group who immediately attached himself to the luckless Cassy—luckless, because he belonged to that irritating, if slightly pathetic, type of male who was of the bigoted opinion that they were irresistible to the opposite sex, and would have been horrified to learn that in actual fact they were crashing bores to be avoided at all costs!

That the austere Aunt Mary had got him weighed up was proved by his sudden switch to Cassy after the party boarded the fleet of taxis waiting to convey them to the chosen club for the evening.

It was bad enough for Cassy to find herself landed with this type of escort, but worse was to come, since the chosen club turned out to be the very same club that Justin had taken her to the previous evening. What with avoiding the very obvious passes being handed out by her self-appointed partner for the evening, and desperately trying not to think of the way she had felt when Justin had sat next to her, Cassy had no chance whatsoever of enjoying the evening; culminating, she thought sourly, with a free-for-all in the taxi on the way back to the hotel at the close of the evening!

She was at least saved this further indignity by the simple fact that there was a shortage of taxis, and each vehicle took on six passengers. Her next worry was how to get rid of this persistent man once they had reached the hotel, and she consoled herself with the fact that although he was staying in the same hotel, he was not in possession of her room number, and Cassy meant things to stay that way.

From now on, she told herself grimly, evening tours were out—the loquacious Reginald Germaine having told her that he had booked all the night club tours, in a manner that suggested that she was very fortunate indeed to find herself such an eligible partner.

When they arrived at the hotel, it was much as Cassy had feared, for her determined admirer, placing one proprietorial arm round her slim waist that she no less determinedly removed, followed her to the lift fully intending, she was sure, to collect what he would consider his due for his constant attention to her welfare that evening. On this thought she swallowed a lump that had suddenly arisen in her throat; she had once mentally accused Justin of trying the very same tactics, but how wrong she had been.

As the lift attendant now knew her, there was no need for her to give her floor number and for this she was thankful, and when her floor was reached she stepped smartly out of the lift, and waving a casual goodnight to the caught-off-balance Reginald, she all but ran to her room, and once inside, locked the door with fingers that trembled slightly, thanking providence for her escape from what might have been a highly embarrassing interlude.

The following morning Cassy ventured down to the desk to find out if Justin had left any message for her the previous evening, and was slightly piqued to find that no message had been left. He had probably taken her earlier advice and found another partner for the evening, and she found the thought hurtful—but that was stupid, she told herself scathingly; she couldn't have it both ways. She had wanted him to leave her alone, hadn't she? The fact that that was precisely what he had done had given her an unpleasant jolt, she had somehow thought ... Her eyes misted over; she was being stupid again. The best thing she could do was to apply her mind to other matters, such as the letter she ought to write to her uncle. Well, she would do that straight away, there was no time like the present.

'Ah, there you are!' came a familiar yet most unwelcome voice at her elbow, and Cassy found the obnoxious Reginald standing beside her. 'I waited for you to put in an appearance at breakfast, but I guess you slept late,' he said in a light, slightly complaining voice, as he gave her what was supposed to be a roguish look, but appeared as a leer to the annoyed Cassy.

'I had breakfast in my room,' she said coldly, in a manner that would have given a more sensitive man a hint of her feelings, but had no impression whatsoever on the man beside her.

'I could do with another cup of coffee,' went on the annoying man, oblivious to all else but his own requirements. 'How about joining me? We could maybe team up for the day; I'm at a bit of a loose end, friends I was expecting to join me haven't put in an appearance yet, but I guess some of the shots they took of the last scene have had to be scrapped and they've had to shoot it again. It's not all plain sailing in the movie world, you know,' he assured her with a toothy grin.

Cassy's sardonic eyes surveyed him coolly; if he was trying to impress her, he'd failed miserably. As her eyes surveyed his well-cut blazer and open-necked blue shirt, with a navy striped cravat at his throat, the thought occurred to her that he was very probably an actor himself—but one that had passed the zenith of his youth, as she saw now that he was quite a bit older than he had seemed last night. The bit about his 'friends' in the movies might have been true or might not, but it did give Cassy an idea of how she might shrug off this persistent man. 'As a matter of fact, I have friends staying on the island.' It was not a lie, only perhaps she should have said 'friend', the others were only acquaintances, but it served her purpose. 'So I'm afraid my time's booked up,' she went on steadily without a trace of conscience, and gave him what she hoped was a consoling smile. 'I do hope your friends turn up soon,' and turning away from him, she collided with a man standing just behind her.

Justin caught her elbow as she staggered back slightly from the collision, but he was not looking at her, he was looking at the man she had been conversing with.

For a second the two men sized each other up, Reginald with a positive gleam of envy in his eyes as he took in Justin's six-foot measurements as against his five feet ten, and the fact that even though dressed in casual clothes he somehow managed to dominate the situation, and made him feel inferior. It was this feeling of inferiority that made him drawl to Cassy, 'Well, thanks anyway for a wonderful evening. You know where to come if you're ever at a loose end again,' and made his departure, leaving Cassy staring after him in silent outrage. The words had been innocent enough, but it was the underlying meaning that could be so easily misinterpreted—as he had meant them to be, she thought furiously.

'So that's why I got no reply when I rang you last night,' said Justin, watching the man's departure through narrowed eyes. His voice was casual, but Cassy sensed an underlying censure in his manner and resented it.

'You know, I wouldn't have thought ...' he began mildly, and as far as Cassy was concerned he had no need to finish the sentence, she was perfectly aware of the trend of his thoughts. 'Did he offer you a screen test?' he asked in that same mild voice.

Cassy's surprise showed in her eyes. 'You know him, then?' she said curiously.

Justin made a grimace. 'Our Reggie has been living on past glories for quite some time. Er—I shouldn't put too much faith in his promises. He was too fond of the good life to make any lasting impression in the movie world. He just hangs around the big names now, usually with some well-endowed widow who's hoping for an introduction to one of the latest heart-throbs.'

Cassy considered this news silently; it was more or less what she had thought, yet she felt a spurt of pity for the man Justin had so accurately summed up. Not only accurately, but pitilessly, and by all accounts Justin had little cause to condemn such behaviour. 'He didn't seem to know you,' she said with a touch of irony in her voice.

Justin's expressive eyebrows shot up at this, and he gave her a quick speculating look before answering laconically, 'Well, that doesn't surprise me. No doubt he'd prefer to forget our last encounter. He had the misfortune to latch himself on to a friend of mine's daughter.'

Seeing his grim expression, Cassy drew her own conclusion about the outcome. The girl was probably one of those star-struck youngsters easily manipulated by the wiles of 'our Reggie' as Justin had named him. Her father would be extremely wealthy, of course, and Justin had probably picked up quite a large remuneration for his intervention. The thought hurt Cassy, even though she knew it was none of her business how Justin made his living, and the plain simple fact that she had fallen in love with him was her bad luck.

The only answer was to steer clear of him, she thought, as she gave him a quick surreptitious look from under the fringe of her dark eyelashes and received a slight shock to find that he was subjecting her to the same scrutiny, but openly so. 'Well?' he said softly. 'Are we going to stand here all day looking at each other? I could suggest a much less populated place for such interesting observances. Collect your hat and your bag, and we'll go in search of it.'

Cassy's cheeks turned a bright red, for there was a certain look in his eye that made her want to head for the hills—alone, that was! Her knees felt decidedly weak as she acknowledged the awesome fact that if she wasn't very careful she would find herself meekly following him out of the hotel to some unknown destination. As Reggie had the power to manipulate a star-struck being, so Justin had the power to manipulate her, and although her heart pleaded with her to accept this one and only chance of pure magic, her head told her she would be a fool to let him know how much he attracted her. Look at her now; her knees were weak and she felt as if she hadn't a bone in her whole body. With just one look Justin Pride could do that to her—and that was in the middle of a busy hotel lobby!

CHAPTER SEVEN

CASSY'S flushed cheeks and over-bright eyes gave their own answer to the waiting observant Justin, and his eyes narrowed as she forced a smile and said calmly, 'It sounds wonderful, but I'm afraid I've already planned my day.' She gave a vague shrug. 'There's a letter I must write,' she went on, hastily avoiding Justin's eyes, 'and to be honest, I do feel lazy. I was looking forward to a few hours on my own.' She gave another expressive shrug. 'Just doing nothing,' she added rather lamely now as she noted the derisive look in his eyes.

'Scared?' he said softly, making the red in Cassy's cheeks turn a deeper hue, and making her want to hit out at him for his astuteness.

'Of course not!' she answered smartly, too smartly, as Justin's slow smile silently acknowledged.

'I'll wait, then,' he said calmly, adding on seeing Cassy's puzzled glance at him, 'till you finish your letter. I feel lazy too.'

So saying he turned her round gently towards the lift, and slipping his hand into the crook of her arm guided her across the lobby. 'Bring plenty of sun lotion,' he advised her conversationally, and it wasn't until the lift appeared and Cassy stepped in that she noted with a pang of panic that Justin was still beside her.

He was taking no chances on her slipping out of the

hotel at the first available opportunity, she thought bitterly—and she had thought the abominable Reginald pushing! There was another thought hovering around at the back of her mind, and one that caused her further palpitations. There was some indefinable tension between her and the silent man by her side that had not been there before, and she sensed a showdown of some kind; perhaps another lecture on her calculating method of ingratiating herself into a moneyed family. If it was just that, Cassy felt she could cope; if it wasn't ...

By the time they reached her room, the tension she felt made her fumble clumsily for the key in the pocket of her jeans, well aware that Justin could not have missed her agitation, and wondering bitterly if he was enjoying putting her on the rack.

Once inside, and with a nonchalance she was far from feeling, Cassy said airily, 'Well, make yourself at home. I don't know how long I shall be, but as you insisted on accompanying me, be it on your own head. And don't ask me to hurry,' she added with a touch of asperity in her voice.

Totally ignoring this last direction, Justin walked over to the window seat and made himself comfortable, but did not look out of the window at the fine view in front of him, but back at the now infuriated Cassy. 'Who's the letter to?' he queried with the confident air of someone entitled to receive an answer, adding to Cassy's fury.

Her flashing eyes said more than words, and this seemed to amuse Justin who waited patiently for an answer. 'I don't see that that's any of your business, do you?' she said baldly, and at the look of reproach she received for this she felt immediately contrite, and hastened to soften her reply by adding, 'I ought to have written it soon after my arrival,' purposely not answering his earlier query.

'Sylvia's father,' he said, more in the nature of a statement than a question. 'What will you tell him?' he asked blandly. 'That she refuses to return?'

Cassy took a deep breath. She could go back to her earlier reply by telling him to mind his own business, yet he had plainly made it his business purely out of kindness for Sylvia—or had he? Or was he hoping for monetary returns for his assistance? Cassy sighed inwardly—if only she really knew! Her heart told her that he was incapable of such mercenary machinations, but she could not trust her heart, not when the man concerned was as attractive as Justin Pride was!

'I shall tell him no such thing!' she said, taking a hold on her emotions. 'Because I think she will return, when she's good and ready, and this I will tell him.' She looked beyond Justin to the view behind his shoulder. 'She's just making a gesture,' she added slowly. 'Oh, I admit the island's wonderful, but she knows she doesn't belong here any more than I do. It's just a nice place to make a stand. I'd give her no more than three months, and she'll be homeward bound. Are you going to see that she gets a job?' she asked bluntly.

Justin's eyebrows lifted at this. 'I don't see that that's necessary now, do you?' he asked mildly. 'Aren't you forgetting something?'

Cassy frowned at the query, then enlightenment came and she gave him a sardonic smile. 'I suppose you're referring to Greg. Well, for all I know it might be just a holiday romance. Sylvia is rather apt to go in at the deep end,' she said a little primly, 'I've seen it before. I'll believe it when it happens—the real thing, I mean.'

Justin sat watching her for a second or two, then said musingly, 'There would be no such dalliances for you, of course, and I wonder why. Frightened to commit yourself—or just frightened of emotion? Is that why you settled for an old man?'

Cassy gasped at the way an ordinary conversation had suddenly turned to such personal issues. 'We were discussing Sylvia,' she replied hotly, 'not me—and Sylvia's father is not an old man,' she added for good measure, visualising her uncle's outraged reaction to this epitaph.

'Forty-five, fifty?' went on Justin in the same musing manner, 'an old man as against your youth. Why don't you stay too? I would look after you. If the idea appealed to you, we could team up.' His eyes pierced Cassy's shocked wide-open eyes. 'Now that does shake you, doesn't it?' he said with a trace of amusement in his voice. 'Are you so used to feeling unwanted that you don't realise just how attractive you are?' His eyes held hers. 'Write that letter,' he said in a soft yet firm voice, 'and tell him to find someone of his own age.'

Cassy felt like shaking her head to clear the fog that had suddenly descended upon her unsuspecting head. She couldn't think straight, yet she had to! Had Justin Pride proposed to her or not? Her befuddled senses tried to reconstruct his words and she couldn't recall anything being said about marriage, apart from a reference to teaming up with him.

Her eyes opened yet wider as a certain implication

made itself felt on her bemused mind. Did he want her to work with him as his accomplice—on whatever dubious schemes he might or might not have in mind? Surely the very meaning of 'team' meant some kind of partnership, and not the matrimonial one she had almost mistaken it for.

She blinked quickly as a surge of bitterness rushed over her. Justin didn't know it, but his reference to her feeling unwanted had touched a chord deep in her heart. Something she had kept locked away in the inner recesses of her being, not wanting to acknowledge it lest it colour her outlook on life. It was only because she had made herself useful that she had been wanted, in any sense. There had been a total lack of affection in her life since she had lost her parents, and until this moment Cassy had refused to remember how bleak those first few months had been in her uncle's home, and how it was the kennels that had lifted her out of her abject misery—and still would, she thought, as she swallowed the lump in her throat and turned her attention to the man watching her so closely, and waiting for her answer to what now appeared to be a very dubious proposal.

There was only one way to tackle this sort of situation, and Cassy took it. 'And lose everything when I'm so close to obtaining my goal?' she asked in a light matter-of-fact voice, and gave the watching Justin a clear direct look. 'Come now, you didn't really expect me to take you up on your offer, did you?' she asked sardonically.

Justin's watching eyes narrowed at her casual rejection, then passed slowly over her slim figure in the close-fitting jeans and open-necked white blouse that she had chosen to wear that day. 'I wonder what you'd do if I made a dead set at you,' he said, adopting the same light tone of voice that Cassy had used.

'I wouldn't advise it,' answered Cassy, feeling her pulse rate soar at the thought. 'You'd only be wasting your time. Mine, too, come to that,' she added coldly.

'That's what I can't fathom about you,' he said quietly. 'I'd swear you're not an old man's darling; unless,' he added in a slow ruminating voice, 'you've had a hard time of it. You are related to Sylvia, aren't you? Sort of second cousin, I think she said.'

Cassy did not reply straight away, but just looked at him with one eyebrow slightly raised, wondering what else he was going to say. He was certainly tenacious! If it helped him to understand her then she would encourage that line of thought; that way she could keep her distance. 'Well, I suppose that's near enough,' she replied slowly, 'and you're right—I did have a hard time of it, and it's not been easy. Why shouldn't I grab what I can?' she said challengingly. 'They owe me that much,' she tacked on fervently, for she was thinking of the kennels, and how she had been at the beck and call of the Mellar family for all those years without anyone realising that she had a right to a life of her own.

Justin's lips tightened as he surveyed her flushed cheeks and bright periwinkle eyes, the blue more emphasised by her emotion, an emotion that highlighted her high cheekbones, giving her features an elfin-like beauty. 'I'll still say you could do better for yourself,' he observed meaningly.

Cassy's heart was now thumping against her rib cage; she was in dangerous waters. 'Oh, I don't think so,' she replied airily. 'Rather the devil you know, as the saying goes,' she quoted lightly, feeling a stab of panic at the look of fury now apparent in his eyes.

'Turning me down, are you?' he asked in a low but perfectly controlled voice that made Cassy wonder if he was testing her out for his own amusement.

The thought gave her the necessary courage to answer him. 'If you put it like that, I suppose I am,' she replied with a glint in her eye. 'As for "doing better" as you've just suggested, I might say the same of you,' she parried in an acid-sweet voice. 'I'm a hanger-on too, remember. All I have is what I manage to salvage for myself, and as attractive as your offer is, I'm not passing up this chance.'

If she had been uncertain of his feelings before, she was now in no doubt that he was absolutely furious. His blazing eyes looked as if they were on fire, and she absently noted the way a small muscle twitched at the side of his firmly moulded mouth as he attempted to get a hold on himself, but his feelings were too strong to contain and he made a swift lunge at her and pulled her into his arms.

Although she tried to release herself, no amount of struggling caused him to relax the iron hold he had on her, and in the end she had to submit weakly to his enforced embrace.

When all the fight had gone out of her, Justin caught the hair at the back of her head, and she found herself jerked back to accept his punishing lips.

It was not a kiss that she enjoyed in any way; she had never been kissed before, but always thought it would be a nice experience providing you wanted to be kissed. It had never occurred to her that it could be a degrading one, but that was the only way she could describe the kiss Justin was subjecting her to. His lips roamed her wide forehead when he had finished pounding her full and now very sore lips.

The kiss had been shattering enough, but when his free hand that held her clamped tight against his body now gently caressed her back, sending tremors through her body, the feelings this deliberate action evoked frightened her far more than his earlier assault had.

She was released without warning, and Justin stood surveying her with hooded lids. 'You'll have to learn to be more compliant,' he ground out between clenched teeth. 'You wouldn't want to disappoint your sugar daddy, would you?' he queried savagely.

Fear was now replaced by fury; Cassy had been made to feel degraded and used, simply because this bullying character had felt the urge to prove his manhood to an inexperienced girl—and what was worse, he now knew she was inexperienced, and in his eyes a rather pathetic go-getter who was trading her innocence for a pot of gold. She ought not to have let things get this far; in a way she had asked for what she had got. Her eyes filled with tears of frustration, and she so badly wanted to hit back at this man who was only playing with her anyway.

'He won't be disappointed,' she managed to get out furiously. 'Do you think I'm stupid enough to play your sort of game? What do you live on anyway? You're only a b-beach Romeo, if the t-truth be known!' she flung out at him, not really realising what she was saying, but only intent on hitting back at him for making her feel cheap.

Justin's narrowed eyes half widened in shock at her

words, and his lean tanned features looked leaner as he drew in a sharp breath. 'Beach Romeo,' he said softly. 'So that's how you see me, is it?'

Cassy looked away quickly from those searching eyes of his, feeling immediately ashamed of herself. Even if she had thought he was a waster, she ought not to have said so—and she wouldn't have done, she told herself miserably, if she hadn't been so upset, but it was too late now, the damage had been done—she knew that much from the look in his eyes.

'So in that case, I've nothing to lose, have I?' he went on in that same soft, yet deadly voice. 'It wouldn't be fair not to pass some of my vast experience on to you. You'll probably thank me later—at least you'll know what to expect on your wedding night,' he added grimly, as he caught her to him again.

Sheer terror made Cassy open her mouth to scream, but the sound never left her lips as Justin's ruthless ones smothered it effectively.

This time the kiss was gentle and even more effective for its seductive quality, and Cassy felt herself go pliant, and to her utter consternation, her arms seemed to act of their own volition and crept up around his neck. From that moment on, Cassy was lost, her whole being offering itself to the man who had so completely mastered her. She no longer felt cheap and used, but very much desired, and had the world at her feet, given her by this man she so desperately loved.

The rosy aura that so completely enfolded her while she was in his arms was shattered in a flash when he threw her away from him, and as she staggered back from the unsuspected move of his, she saw the mockery and triumph in his eyes as he coolly surveyed her, breathless and partially dazed. 'Taking a leaf out of Reggie's book,' he said sardonically. 'You know where to find me if you're at a loose end,' and he walked out of the room.

Cassy stood staring at the door, and drew in a ragged breath. Should she be foolish enough to take him up on his offer, she knew only too well that he would not be available. His cold eyes had told her that, and more besides, she thought as she swallowed a lump in her throat.

With legs that threatened to collapse under her, she walked over to the chair by the window and sat down. Her eyes were blind to the view in front of her as she willed herself to remain calm. So she had made an all-time fool of herself, so what? She wouldn't be the last woman to suffer such an indignity, particularly at the hands of such an old hand at the game as Justin Pride. Her eyes travelled slowly over her trembling hands and she clenched them together in an effort to stop the trembling.

When Cassy had got over the initial shock of her devastating encounter with Justin, her first instinct was to search out the pushing Reginald Germaine and ingratiate herself back into his good books again. She knew she could do it; it would be a sop to his pride that he would willingly accept, and she could rely on Sylvia to innocently pass the news on to Justin. The thought of his reaction gave her a much needed shot in the arm, for in his way he was just as vulnerable as the other man, particularly as she had turned him down.

However appealing this idea was, after a few moments' reflection it appeared not quite so desirable. Why should she suffer another such evening in the company of that puffed-up specimen, just to get her own back on the autocratic Justin? She drew in a deep breath; he wasn't worth it! Besides that, he was extremely astute. Cassy did not know how much of her conversation with Reginald Germaine he had overheard, but it must have been obvious that she was handing out what was popularly labelled as the 'brush-off'.

The phone in her room rang, shrilly piercing through her troubled musings, and she stared at it malevolently. She didn't want to talk to anyone. It was probably Sylvia, and she didn't feel up to listening to her rapturous comments on how she was enjoying life at the present moment. Perhaps it would stop if she just sat tight, but it did not, and the persistent buzzing forced her reluctantly to answer it.

It was not Sylvia, but her father, and Cassy gave a sigh of exasperation as his high-pitched complaining voice came over the line to her; she could have done without his bullying reminder of why she was there.

'Have you seen Sylvia?' he demanded in that impatient voice of his. 'I was expecting to hear from you before now,' he complained sourly.

'Yes, I've seen her,' she answered wearily. 'And I think she needs a little more time to think things over.'

'Think what over?' he asked aggressively. 'Did you tell her she'll get no more money from me until she returns?' he demanded.

'I think she knows that,' returned the exasperated Cassy, then remembering Greg, she added slowly, 'but there's a little more to it now.'

'I knew it!' he said in a triumphant voice. 'She's got herself mixed up with someone, hasn't she? Some thoroughly undesirable type. What's his name?'

'Greg Storn,' replied Cassy, having a hard time holding on to her temper, 'and he's not an undesirable type. Quite presentable, as a matter of fact. A golfer, and very highly thought of in the States. If you don't believe me, you could check him out,' knowing that that was exactly what he would do.

'Hmph!' was her uncle's only response while he thought about this. 'Not too sure that I ought not to make the trip out myself,' he grumbled, now slightly more placated. 'Think it's serious, do you?' he barked out at Cassy.

How could she answer this? she thought sardonically. Sylvia thought so. She hedged a little. 'According to Sylvia, yes,' she said carefully.

Her uncle caught the hesitation in her voice and pounced on it. 'But you're not convinced?' he shot out at her. 'I think I'd better make that trip out, after all,' he threatened.

Cassy took a deep sigh. To be honest, she wouldn't have minded in the least if he did just that; she had been on the receiving end for long enough. It would also, she thought with a justifiable spurt of malice, clear the air all round, and the clever Mr Pride would have to eat a certain amount of humble pie after he had had a few stern words with Sylvia. 'That's entirely up to you,' she said calmly.

'Well, we'll see,' muttered her uncle. 'Couldn't have come at a worse time,' he grumbled. 'Having some trouble with some shareholders who think we ought to amalgamate with a Swedish firm.'

Cassy listened, but did not take much notice of the remarks. Business did not interest her, that was her uncle's domain. She knew what he meant by his 'We'll see,' though. He would check on Greg, and if satisfied of his bona fides, then he would sit on the fence and await results, and rely on Cassy to keep an eye on the situation.

'I'll get her to write to you,' she said, now with a weary note in her voice as her fond vision of his appearance in the very near future faded into oblivion.

'Yes, you do that,' answered her uncle, a note of relief in his voice. 'I can rely on you, you're a good girl,' he ended in a placatory tone, and put his receiver down before she could answer.

Cassy replaced her receiver slowly. He hadn't once asked if she was enjoying herself, and though this omission would not have caused her any heartache previously, as she was well used to such treatment, it now touched a raw spot in her heart. As her eyes misted over, she had to admit that she had become vulnerable. Vulnerable to what she had carefully armoured herself against all these years, getting used to being called a 'good girl' through her usefulness to her uncle, but no loving hug for her, or genuine anxiety to see to her happiness. She was just part of the furniture, serving a purpose and pushed aside when she had served that purpose—or at least she would have been had it not been for the kennels.

The kennels! she thought with a spurt of exasperation. Her uncle hadn't said one word about the purchase, and wasn't that just like him! She bit her soft lip on the thought that it was typical of her uncle to conveniently forget any other business but his own, but not typical of her. There had been plenty of time for her to have made the enquiry as to how things were progressing and whether he had made the transaction.

She walked over to the bed and sat down on it shakily. What had happened to her? How could she have let such an opportunity pass? It was as if she had passed into another dimension of time, and what had gone before had no significance for her. She shook her head blindly; was this what happened when one fell in love? she wondered in a daze. Had Justin Pride so filled her being that she was oblivious to all else? And what of the future? Cassy thought with a quick inward breath that turned into a raw sob as she envisaged the bleakness ahead of her, she had no future! Not now, only an existence, and if Sylvia married Greg —She got up from the bed abruptly; she wouldn't think about that. But she did think about it, and found herself fervently hoping that no such alliance would come about. Selfish or no, she couldn't help her feelings on this, for their happiness would be a constant reminder of her unhappiness and what might have been.

Might have been? She frowned as she repeated the words silently to herself. What might have been? Was she going soft in the head? And wasn't it time she pulled herself together? Anyone would think Justin had proposed to her instead of suggesting some dubious team-up. She brushed away a stray tear angrily; it was this island, it must be! She wasn't normally like this; when she got home she would look back on all this with a certain amount of incredulity and wonder what had come over her. She nodded her head vigorously; of course she would! As for the future, she had every reason to look forward to it with great anticipation. She would be free at last from the beck and call of the Mellar family, and so would Sylvia. How selfish of her not to wish for Sylvia's happiness simply because she had very nearly made a fool of herself over a man who lived on his wits—a grasper of opportunities, who probably had a whole string of women pining for his company. Well, she could count herself lucky that she had had the presence of mind to escape embroilment with him.

Cassy felt decidedly better after this little lecture she had given herself, and when her phone rang again, and Sylvia's voice came over the line, she was able to talk to her with an equability that surprised her.

'Hi!' said Sylvia gaily. 'Greg's in the final, how about that!' she enthused happily. 'Justin's returned today, so I expect he'll be contacting you. Did you enjoy yourself last night?' she asked the now scowling Cassy, who was about to answer this query in no uncertain manner, then decided it might be better if everyone thought she was enjoying herself—including Justin Pride! She also thought it best not to mention that she had seen Justin; the less said about that encounter, the better.

'Yes, thank you,' she lied stoutly. 'Had a wonderful time. Got myself booked for the rest of the week,' she perjured herself further, on the excuse that it was all in a good cause.

'Oh dear, Justin won't like that,' replied Sylvia with a hint of amusement in her voice. 'He made a point of finding out if I remembered to ring you yesterday and cancel your date.'

Cassy's hand clenched on the receiver. 'Oh, I expect he'll survive,' she said, trying to insert a gay note into her voice, but her earlier revival of spirits suffered a setback, and she was beginning to feel miserable again.

In an effort to change the conversation she asked, 'When's the final?'

Her tactics worked as she had known they would, and for the next few minutes Sylvia enthused on the merits of Greg's dexterity on the golf course, ending up with, 'Well, I suppose I shall see you some time. Tell you what, keep Saturday free for us. We'll have dinner together—at least, with Greg and me. I can't speak for Justin, of course, but I'll mention it to him, if you want me to?'

The question was idly asked, yet Cassy caught the hopeful note in it, as if she was trying to instil some kind of conscience into Cassy for being so unhelpful, and so antagonistic towards someone who had helped Sylvia so much.

Cassy, however, was not to be drawn into such a trap, knowing full well that even if he were asked, he would turn the invitation down, arousing Sylvia's curiosity still further, and that was something Cassy wanted to avoid at all costs. 'Don't bother to ask Justin,' she said quickly. 'Just make it you, me and Greg, in case I decide to bring my own partner—if you see what I mean,' she went on as gaily as she could manage. On those terms Sylvia could hardly ask Justin to join them.

There was a short silence the other end as Sylvia digested this, then she said curiously, 'So it's like that, is it? I think you'd better bring him along. I want to see this man who appears to have got through that load of armour you've been skulking behind all these years.'

Alarmed, Cassy replied hastily, 'Oh, it's nothing like that. He's just good fun.' She closed her eyes on having to give yet another downright lie. 'Besides, I might have had enough of his company by Saturday, so I'd much rather you left things open,' she instructed.

Sylvia reluctantly gave her word on this, but the curiosity was still in her voice as she ended with, 'Well, enjoy yourself. See you Saturday.'

Replacing the receiver with a sigh, Cassy wondered if she would ever be in a position to unfurl the tangle she was in. Things got worse instead of better. In trying to get herself out of one awkward situation, she had landed herself in another. For goodness' sake, why had she to bring another odd character into the ménage? She ought to have just asked Sylvia to make it a three-some, and left it at that, and she would have done if she hadn't been so certain that Sylvia would approach Justin, in spite of Cassy's feelings on the matter.

The next thing Cassy did was to cancel all the tours she had booked; explaining to the slightly surprised booking clerk that she had met a friend on the island, and had decided to join forces with her for the rest of her holiday, and at the apologetic but firm reply that they were unable to give her a refund on the bookings, she assured them that she had not expected any such remuneration, and left the counter with the booking clerk's kindly, 'Have a good day,' wishes, that were well meant but hardly likely, thought Cassy caustically.

Going back to her room, she collected her hat and bag and left the hotel, deliberately making herself unavailable for any further calls, in person or phone-wise, since she felt she had had her quota of unwelcome surprises for that day and planned to browse around the shopping precincts of Nassau, having lunch out, and returning to the hotel later, to spend the rest of the day on the beach.

CHAPTER EIGHT

Cassy was fortified by a few hours' peace, and an interesting survey of the wonders of a tropical island's offerings, not only in the shopping precincts, but the harbour activity where she watched the local fishermen unload their fascinating catches. She would have stayed longer had she not seen that one of the boats a little further up had brought in a giant turtle. She felt saddened at the necessity to capture such a harmless creature, and walked away. Not even the knowledge that the turtle provided food, and its shell was used to make items of jewellery that provided yet another source of income to the islanders, helped to assuage her feelings on this. She liked turtles—she couldn't help that, could she? she argued silently to herself as she waved a cruising taxi down and went back to the hotel.

The afternoon tours had left by the time she returned, and all was quiet in the usually hectic reception area. Cassy was just congratulating herself on the success of her plan to keep in the background when she was confronted by a grinning Sylvia who must have been waiting in the hotel foyer until her return.

Feeling very frustrated, Cassy was forced to try and appear pleased to see her, but it was not easy. The girls went up to Cassy's room, Sylvia babbling on about one thing and another, and Cassy, not missing the way she kept looking around the foyer on Cassy's

arrival, knew she had been hoping to meet the man
who had captured Cassy's own interest. It was sheer
curiosity that had torn her away from Greg's side for
a few hours, and though irritated, Cassy felt a spurt of
remorse for misleading her, until she reminded herself
that it was all Sylvia's fault anyway. If she had been
honest at the start, Cassy wouldn't be in this predica-
ment.

Out of the corner of her eye she eyed the exuber-
ant Sylvia, noting the added sparkle in her eyes making
her look positively lovely, and had to acknowledge with
a pang in her heart that she was well and truly in love.
There was a kind of shy yet complete assurance about
her that Cassy had not seen before—the kind of assurance that came when a person knew that their love was
returned. She swallowed hastily on the thought. Sylvia
had apparently landed on her feet; the path ahead was
strewn with rose petals. Well, it would be, once everything was straightened out with her father.

This thought led to another. 'I had a phone call
from your father,' she said, as she inserted the key into
the lock opening the door of her room and ushering
Sylvia in. 'He threatened to come out here,' she added
dryly.

Sylvia's eyebrows rose as she queried, 'Well? Is he
coming?'

Cassy gave her a long considering look. Once upon
a time, in actual fact a little over forty-eight hours ago,
such a communication would have had Sylvia rushing
out to find some kind of sanctuary from her father's
bullying presence. In spite of her earlier statement
that she hoped that he would put in an appearance, she
must have known that it would mean the end of her

charade. Now here she was, casually querying whether he was coming or not, as if he was some acquaintance who might or might not drop in on them! She sighed inwardly; it was just another sign of Sylvia's new-found confidence, bolstered by the thought of her brawny Greg protecting his love!

'He might have done,' she replied, feeling a spurt of pure envy at Sylvia's rose-coloured world. 'I told him about Greg,' she went on, swallowing her feelings. 'No doubt he's looking him up in Who's Who—or some such informative journal. So if he's as celebrated a character as you say, you've nothing to worry about. He also has trouble with the shareholders,' she tacked on dryly, with a hint of amusement in her voice, for they were both aware of Sylvia's father's obsession that the company would collapse without his personal guidance, and even on holiday he would keep in close touch with head office.

Sylvia grinned appreciatively at this. 'Well, I can't say I'm sorry,' she said impishly. 'I'm expecting Greg to pop the question any day now. He wants to,' she said, with a loving look in her eye, 'but I think he's afraid it's too soon, and is just biding his time. I've a feeling he'll do it after he's won the final,' she confided happily to Cassy.

Not 'if he wins the final', noted Cassy, now back to the envious stage. Even if he lost, it wouldn't make any difference, of that she was now certain. Lucky Sylvia! 'I told your father you would write to him,' she told Sylvia, glad of a chance to change the conversation as she felt depression creeping over her.

'Oh, dear,' sighed Sylvia, brought back from her happy musings. 'Yes, I suppose I ought to, but I'd rather wait until I have some definite news for him.'

'Well, that's up to you,' commented Cassy, suddenly tired of the whole business.

There was a short silence, then Sylvia burst out, 'Well? Who is he?' in a strangled voice that showed how impatient she was to hear the answer.

It took a moment or so for Cassy to get the trend of her thoughts, and she blinked in puzzlement while she worked the question out.

'Oh, for goodness' sake,' cried Sylvia. 'Who's this mysterious character who's taking up all your spare time? And don't look so innocent. I mean to find out,' she threatened. 'He must be some kind of superman if you prefer him to Justin,' she went on musingly, 'particularly as Justin is interested in you. I did tell you so, but you wouldn't believe me. Greg and I were talking to him just before I came over here, and Greg said something about you having a heavy date. He was only teasing, you know, but Justin looked like thunder, and I had to give Greg a slight kick on the ankle to shut him up.'

Cassy looked away quickly. Sylvia didn't know the half of it! What would she say if she were to tell her what had happened between herself and Justin that very morning? 'What does Justin do for a living?' she asked, to give herself time to answer Sylvia's previous question.

Sylvia started, and stared at Cassy, then gave a half surprised snort. 'Of all the people I might have accused of being snobbish, you'd be the last,' she said in an indignant voice. 'So that's what's worrying you, is it? And you asked me that question before, didn't you?' she added accusingly.

'Only because I was afraid he was helping you for purely monetary reasons,' replied Cassy wearily.

Sylvia surveyed her out of narrowed eyes. 'And why are you asking now?' she demanded suspiciously.

Cassy looked away from her searching eyes; she would have to be careful now. 'Because I'm interested,' she said bluntly, and seeing a gleam of speculation in Sylvia's eyes, added quickly, 'Not that way. I just can't understand how he comes to be doing nothing, yet suddenly takes off on a business trip—at least, I suppose it was a business trip,' she amended lamely.

Sylvia continued to survey her for a second or two in silence, and try as she might, Cassy could not prevent the telltale pink flush from creeping into her cheeks.

'Shall I tell you what I think?' said Sylvia softly, but triumphantly. 'I think you're more than just interested in him. You've fallen for him, haven't you? And you're terrified he might be some sort of beachcomber! Shame on you, Cassy! If it weren't for Greg I'd have a good stab at grabbing him for myself. Well,' she amended ruefully, 'I would have done, if given half the chance.'

'What nonsense!' retorted Cassy in a firm voice that she hoped would fool Sylvia. 'If he wouldn't look at you, he certainly wouldn't look at me. We're two little girls as far as he's concerned. All right, so he's interested in me—but that's as far as it goes. I'm not so green that I can't see that.' She altered her approach in an effort to make Sylvia understand how it was. 'Look, dear,' she said quietly. 'In a few days' time I shall be catching a plane home. Just supposing—and I mean supposing—that I did fall in love with him. Oh, I admit I'm attracted to him, I'll concede that much, but where will that get me? I'll also admit that I'm frightened of him, frightened of the attraction he holds for me, and I don't intend to spend the rest of my life sighing for someone I can't have. Does that make sense to you or not?' she asked in a low voice.

Sylvia was immediately contrite. 'Oh, Cassy,' she wailed, 'and I teased you so much, didn't I?'

Cassy looked away. So much for her hoping she could fool Sylvia! She ought to have known that they were too close to each other for any such tactics.

'But how do you know he isn't serious?' Sylvia asked suddenly, a brighter note entering her voice. 'He did look put out when Greg remarked about your absence from the scene, and then mentioned you having a heavy date—and that was my fault, I told him about the man you said you'd met.' She gave Cassy a searching look. 'I suppose that was a story you made up to keep Justin away, was it?' she asked.

Cassy walked over to the window and stood looking out at the bright vista before she replied, 'It was partially true. I did meet someone on the one and only evening tour I participated in. The only deviation being that he was a crashing bore who clung like a limpet to me all evening. He was even waiting for me to have breakfast with him, in spite of the fact that I'd done everything possible the previous evening to show him that he was wasting his time, and would he please go and pick on someone else. I was politely repeating the message to him this morning when Justin appeared on the scene.'

'Justin came over here this morning?' interrupted Sylvia in a surprised voice. 'He didn't mention it.'

Cassy closed her eyes; she hadn't wanted Sylvia to

know that, but it was too late now. She gave a weary sigh. Sylvia might as well know the whole of it. At least it would help her to understand Cassy's attitude towards him. She turned to face Sylvia and gave a wry smile. 'No, I don't suppose he saw the necessity, particularly as I said no to a certain proposition he had in mind.'

'Proposition!' squeaked Sylvia with wide eyes. 'For goodness' sake, what kind of proposition?'

'I didn't bother to enquire,' replied Cassy sardonically. 'Apart from the fact that he thought we might "team up" together, and asked me to stay on here.'

Sylvia sat down weakly on the nearest chair. 'Could it have been a kind of proposal?' she said wonderingly.

'Oh, it was a proposal all right,' replied Cassy ironically, 'but not the marriage sort, if you see what I mean.'

Sylvia was decidedly shaken. 'Who'd have thought,' she muttered, then looked back at Cassy. 'Cassy,' she said firmly, 'I think you ought to take the first plane out of here,' in a motherly way that made Cassy want to smile in spite of the tight ache in her heart.

She gave her cousin a smile. 'Rest easy, dear. He might be fascinating, but I'm not that stupid. I'm sure he won't bother me again. That was why he was so furious when your Greg dropped that brick. I mean, it must have been galling for him; I shouldn't think he's had many refusals in the past, would you?'

Sylvia did not reply as she was deep in thought, and she chewed her lower lip for a few seconds. 'Perhaps it makes sense after all,' she cogitated to herself, and in a still wondering voice added, 'He's not a beach-comber, Cassy. In fact, he's a very wealthy man. He owns the Beach Hotel, and several other hotels on the out islands. Greg told me about him,' she gave Cassy an apologetic look. 'I could have told you before, only I was a bit cross with you for not accepting him as he was, or the sort of person you seemed to think he was,' she amended hastily. 'But Greg did say something else; something about the way women chased him, and how he was a little too clever to get caught. So I expect ...' She did not finish the sentence, she had no need to as Cassy was well aware of the trend of her thoughts.

'And as I belonged to that same category of fortune-hunters that he so abhors, or at least as you had alleged I did, he thought I was fair game. I suppose,' Cassy said slowly, 'he was attracted by my firm refusal to play the game. Probably thought it was some kind of come-on. At least, until he called my bluff, as he did this morning.' Cassy omitted to mention that she had called him a 'beachcomber'!

'So that's that!' said Sylvia in a despondent voice. 'It's all my fault,' she sighed miserably. 'If I'd owned up and told the truth earlier, none of this would have happened,' she gulped. 'He might have fallen for you,' she sniffed loudly. 'He was interested right from the start, I knew he was!'

'Oh, I doubt it,' answered Cassy consolingly. 'For goodness' sake don't blame yourself on that score. If I'd been a nice respectable girl, he wouldn't have looked twice at me. There's nothing remarkable about me, and you know it!' she said half jocularly. 'He told me himself he couldn't make me out, and that he didn't see me as an old man's darling.'

'That proves my point,' wailed Sylvia, refusing to be consoled. She gave another loud sniff, then sat up straight. 'I'm going to tell him the truth,' she said, 'and he can jolly well apologise to you!' she declared firmly.

'You'll do no such thing!' answered Cassy in alarm, wondering how she could make Sylvia understand her feelings on this without letting her know that she had fallen in love with Justin. 'Look, dear,' she began earnestly, 'I know how you feel, and I'm grateful, but don't you see that to tell the truth now would put not only yourself, but me and Justin, in a horribly embarrassing position? I backed up your story, remember, so in a way it's not surprising that he propositioned me in that way. And there is another way of looking at it,' she added gently, but firmly. 'The same goes for him as it did for me, doesn't it? What I'm saying is that if he really thought anything about me—gold-digger or no—if he was really serious, is what I'm trying to say, he would hardly have gone that way about things, would he? So be a love, and let things be. I've fixed things my end, and I'm pretty certain he won't bother me again, and that's the way I want it. Promise?' she urged the reluctant Sylvia, who gave a miserable nod in agreement.

'When's the final?' she asked quickly, to take Sylvia's mind off her troubles.

Sylvia made an effort to throw off her despondency. 'Tomorrow,' she answered glumly, then swallowed. 'It doesn't seem fair,' she began miserably.

Cassy could see her dilemma, and broke into her musings with a quick, 'I'd like to watch it. Would you mind if I came?' she queried lightly.

Sylvia gave her a surprised stare. 'Of course not! We'd love you to come.' Her earlier solemnity disappeared as a certain thought struck her. 'I can chew your nails after I get down to the quicks of mine,' she said with a grin. 'It's stupid really, I'm certain Greg's going to win, but I keep getting those blown up mirages of him floundering in a sand pit!'

Relieved, Cassy grinned back at her. 'I expect he has a few of those himself,' she said. 'They're called bunkers, aren't they?'

'In more ways than one!' laughed Sylvia.

Sylvia stayed to take tea with Cassy, and left her just after six to have dinner with Greg, promising to pick her up at ten the following morning in good time to watch the match. Before she left she demanded to know what Cassy was going to do that evening, and Cassy, suspecting that she was going to ask her to join them for dinner, replied hastily that she did not intend to stir outside the hotel. After dinner, she would shut herself in her room and read one of the intriguing-looking paperbacks she hadn't had a chance to read before, and honestly, she was tired.

Not utterly convinced, Sylvia prepared to take her leave. 'Just remember to lock your door,' she advised Cassy, as she gathered up her bag and took a quick look towards the dressing-table mirror to ensure that her appearance was presentable, for Greg was picking her up.

Cassy stared back at her. For goodness' sake, did she think Justin would force his attentions on her? It was mainly the thought of Greg waiting for Sylvia, and what she might say to him, that made her reply hastily, 'I could be wrong, you know——' halting Sylvia in the act of opening the door, and she turned and looked back at Cassy.

'He could,' Cassy went on slowly, but firmly, 'have

been offering me a job, too.' She swallowed. 'Perhaps he was trying to help me, as he helped you,' she added, 'and I took it the wrong way.' Her eyes held a pleading look as they held Sylvia's slightly sceptical ones. 'It could have been a case of wishful thinking on my part,' she said through gritted teeth. No matter what it cost her, she had to convince Sylvia.

By the look of sudden consternation on Sylvia's face, Cassy had succeeded beyond her wildest dreams, for there were tears in Sylvia's eyes as she exclaimed, 'Oh, Cassy! . .' and fled.

There was a hint of tears in Cassy's eyes too, as she picked up one of the paperbacks and settled herself on the bed, determined to lose herself in the labyrinth of a detective story.

However, it was soon apparent that not even the skilful writing of her favourite author could hold her attention from the eventful happenings of the day, and she was forced to discard the book, and lay back on the bed giving her thoughts free rein.

What had Sylvia told Greg? she wondered. Did he know the whole of it? She shook her head slowly; somehow she didn't think he did. There wouldn't have been any necessity for her to mention the way she had hoodwinked Justin into finding a job for her. Not at first, that was, but things were different now, and she would have to tell him some time or other, probably right now, mused Cassy. She would have to have some explanation as to why she was so upset, and if Cassy was any judge of the way she had felt when she had rushed out of the room, she knew she would have flung herself into Greg's arms and confessed all.

On this thought, Cassy tried to assess Greg's re-

action, and whether he would insist on Sylvia 'coming
clean', as it were, and straightening everything out between Cassy and Justin. And where would that lead
them? she wondered. Would Justin renew his interest
in her? As she remembered the way he had flung her
from him, she felt the heat rise in her cheeks. He'd
vanish off the scene so fast he'd break the sound bar-
rier, she told herself caustically. Dealing with a go-
getter, and dealing with an apparently harmless, un-
sophisticated country girl, were two entirely different
things and not easily adjusted to, particularly as she
had more or less insulted him by calling him a beachcomber!

Cassy sighed, and put her arms up under her head.
She would like to apologise to him for that. Even so,
it still didn't completely exonerate his behaviour that
morning. Of course, she admitted a little reluctantly to
herself, she did goad him, but she had seen no other
way to handle the situation. She was not experienced
enough to know how to keep him at a distance.

Her soft lips formed a moue at this thought—would
any woman have been able to? Or come to that, have
wanted to? Little girls baited boys they were interested in like that. Had she unconsciously carried out
the same tactics? She sighed; there was no denying
that she had been disappointed at Justin's failure to
respond to what could have been called a romantic
interlude on the plateau that night.

Which only went to show, she told herself scathingly, what a first-class fool she was. In all probability
her parting remarks to Sylvia that she might be wrong
about Justin's intentions were very likely correct, and
he had only been offering her a job, in which case it

was small wonder that he had reacted the way he had. He might even have gone to the trouble of finding her a job, and for his trouble had received not only a blunt refusal, but a smarting insult thrown in for good measure!

Cassy's brow furrowed as she tried to recall his exact words, but eventually she had to give it up, since she could recall only the 'team up' sentence, and something about if the idea appealed to her. He'd also said something about a 'sugar daddy', she remembered. Her teeth caught her bottom lip and caused her to wince in pain, reminding her of Justin's punishing kiss. No wonder she could not recall much of what went before. The savage pressure of his ruthless mouth on hers had driven all else from her mind.

Cassy sighed in annoyance. Thinking about it had brought her no nearer to an understanding—if anything, to more perplexity. Perhaps it was as well that the whole thing was straightened out. If Justin had attempted to proposition her into some dubious alliance, he was in for a rude awakening! Either way, she told herself reasonably, she had reached the stage where enough was enough, and if he did apologise—well, so would she.

On this comforting thought she picked up the book again, and this time was soon lost in the machinations of a rather celebrated sleuth.

CHAPTER NINE

A VERY bright and cheerful Sylvia called for Cassy the following morning, and giving her a quick speculating look, Cassy wondered what had happened to give her such an uplift, particularly after her downcast exit the previous evening, and suspected it had something to do with a clear conscience!

It was wonderful, she mused as she got into the taxi that Sylvia had requested to wait for her while she picked up Cassy, what a difference love can make, particularly with an understanding, not to mention doting, lover!

In between answering Sylvia's gay comments on everything and nothing in particular, that may or may not have been nerves on Sylvia's part on Greg's behalf, the fact was gradually borne in on Cassy that whatever advice Greg had given Sylvia she was not going to impart it to Cassy, and this somewhat annoyed her. She was as much involved as Sylvia was, more in fact, considering she had been on the receiving end since her arrival.

After a few minutes' thought on this annoying state of affairs, Cassy decided that perhaps it was for the best. She had wanted to be done with the whole charade, hadn't she? Sylvia's determined silence on the matter showed that she and Greg were obviously of the same opinion. Cassy had been made to take the part of the scapegoat for far too long, and they intended to put things right for her.

Even so, she mused silently as the taxi drew up in the forecourt of the luxurious Beach Hotel, she would have liked to have heard Justin's reaction to the news.

As it was the final of the golf tournament, there was much activity inside the hotel, and as Cassy's feet sank into the deep soft pile of the reception lobby, she looked around her with a certain amount of curiosity that stemmed purely from the knowledge that Justin owned the hotel. Not only this one, she thought, but several others, and the fact that he was probably a millionaire did nothing to lessen her chagrin at the thought that she had accused him of living on his wits.

Although Cassy kept a wary eye out for Justin, she did not see him. Not even when the tournament officials presented the cup to the grinning Greg a little before four that afternoon, and she did wonder whether he was deliberately avoiding coming into contact with her. She was now certain that Sylvia had made her rather belated confession to him, so this was not surprising, and in a way Cassy was relieved, for she had some qualms that she, too, might very well come under stricture from Justin for her part in the fictitious story.

As time went by and there was still no sign of Justin, Cassy began to feel a little piqued. He was still on the island, at least she thought he was—must have been, for Sylvia to have seen him earlier, and Cassy was quite sure that she had seen him that day. Not that she had said so in so many words, but the way she had twice squeezed her arm and said in a slightly mysterious voice, 'It's going to be all right, Cassy,' gave Cassy a hint of what had gone before. She also knew that

Sylvia was longing to put her into the picture, but surmised that Greg had insisted on Cassy being left in ignorance of this latest move to put things right.

It was Greg's motive that slightly worried Cassy; if he was simply trying to save her further embarrassment, then it was a praiseworthy action on his part, but if he was looking at it from the romantic involvement angle, then his decision was far more embarrassing for Cassy than the open approach could ever be, since it would be Justin he was looking out for, not Cassy!

With these nebulous thoughts darting about in her head, and Justin's non-appearance, Cassy was only too pleased when the congratulations and hand-shaking bestowed on the triumphant Greg came to an end. They were then able to make their way back to the hotel where tea had been apparently laid on, and was bound to be laced with yet more congratulations, and several speeches thrown in for good measure, thought a thoroughly despondent Cassy, who was determined to make her escape as soon as possible.

To her surprise, Sylvia made no demur when she asked her if she minded if she gave the celebration tea a miss, but when she made the stipulation that Cassy was to have dinner with them that evening, Cassy could not very well refuse, although she had a good try at it. 'Surely you'll want to be alone with Greg,' she said hopefully, and her spirits dropped as Sylvia shook her head decisively.

'I want you to be with us, Cassy,' she said simply, and there was no answer to that, not put in that way.

When Cassy arrived back at her hotel, she went in search of some liquid refreshment in the form of a pot of tea to revive her flagging spirits, and found a fashion show in progress in the large lounge where teas were being served, and sat down to enjoy the show.

After watching several ethereal-looking models gliding about in flimsy gossamer dresses, the prices of which were given as each dress was shown, it occurred to her that she might purchase one of them. That heavenly amber one for example, she thought, as she studied the lovely dress now being shown. It was her colouring, and even though the neckline was a little lower than she would normally think of wearing, it was such a beautiful dress that she could not resist it.

It came as no surprise when she made enquiries about the dress after the show to learn that it was her size. Somehow she had known it would be, and as she tried it on in the makeshift dressing room reserved for such purposes, Cassy felt as if the dress had been made for her. So did the enthusiastic owner of the salon who had put the show on. 'Honey, that sure looks good on you!' she commented in a voice that showed her satisfaction, and frowned as her eye caught an extremely stout lady struggling into a dress that at a rough guess was one size too small for her, and gave a sigh of exasperation at her sales assistant's brief but telling gesture of hunched shoulders and outstretched hands, as if to say, 'I told her so, but she insisted on trying it on.'

The price of the dress was more than Cassy had ever paid for a dress before, but she consoled herself with the thought that she had not bought anything else of value on the island, and looking back at her reflection in the long mirror, decided that it was well worth the price.

The dress was packed up for her, and with a feeling of having unearthed treasure, she made her way back to her room with her purchase. She immediately unpacked it and spread it on the bed for a further appraisal, then feeling a little like Cinderella, she sat and gazed at the full richness of the foamy gossamer skirt with its deeper amber silk underskirt that shone through the gauzy folds whenever the light caught it, making the dress shimmer in a haze of amber sparks.

When her eyes rested on the plunging neckline, she frowned and wondered whether she could put the flimsy neck scarf to a better use, such as somehow arranging it so that it covered the ample cleavage, and nodded to herself. Yes, she ought to be able to manage that.

A quick glance at her watch told her she had exactly one hour and thirty minutes to spare before Greg and Sylvia picked her up for what Sylvia had termed as the 'celebration dinner'. Time enough, she mused, to get her hair set, if she could get an appointment straight away.

Cassy rang the number listed as the hairdressing salon, and made her request. To her delight she got an appointment straight away, and with a definite feeling that for once things were going right for her, set off for the salon.

By the time she got back to her room, she had just twenty minutes in which to get ready for the dinner, ample time really, she thought as she took a quick shower and started to dress.

With the dress on, Cassy set about covering up the plunging neckline with the flimsy scarf, but somehow couldn't get it to look right. Then with firmed lips she arranged the scarf as it was supposed to be worn across her peach-tinted neck, and floating down behind her back. 'After all, it's only once in a lifetime,' she muttered to herself, and it did look right, even though she felt half naked. 'The trouble with you, my girl,' she admonished herself in front of the mirror, 'is that you really are a little country girl. There's a time and a place for everything. Blouses and jeans are all very well for the kennels, but over here it's a case of "when in Rome" and it's not really as bad as all that. Bikinis are lower than this, for a start,' she reminded herself stoutly.

Cassy was ready well before the appointed time, and she spent the waiting minutes in an agony of indecision about wearing the dress, but Sylvia's appreciative gasp of, 'It's beautiful, Cassy, where did you get it?' somewhat eased her mind.

'Here, in the hotel,' answered Cassy a little shakily. 'It's a little low in front, isn't it?' she appealed to Sylvia. 'Do you think I ought . . .' was as far as she got.

'Don't you dare change it for that blouse and skirt,' threatened Sylvia. 'I've a feeling I've just arrived in the nick of time. You were going to change it, weren't you?' she accused her lightly, then smiled at her. 'Pet, you look good enough to eat! If I wasn't so sure of my Greg, I might have a few qualms on sharing our special evening with you!' she added gaily. 'Now, come on, before you have any second thoughts on the matter.'

Half amused, but not wholly confident, Cassy found herself rushed out of her room at great speed, only just remembering to pick up her handbag lying on the side table.

A few minutes later she found herself sitting in the

back of a taxi with Sylvia beside her, Greg having elected to sit up front with the driver. 'Greg thought it better not to use his car,' commented Sylvia with a chuckle. 'We're celebrating, and want to get back in one piece!'

As the taxi sped through the busy town of Nassau, and out towards the Beach Hotel, Cassy wondered if the celebration dinner was going to be held at their hotel, for the taxi was definitely heading that way, but if so, there had been no need for the pair of them to pick her up, nor for Sylvia's remarks concerning Greg not wanting to drive, so it had to be somewhere else, somewhere along the coast, she mused, as she caught sight of twinkling lights out at sea as they passed the imposing front entrance of the Beach Hotel and continued along a coastal road.

Cassy did notice that they met no other traffic, and had not done so since they had passed the Beach Hotel, and she had a feeling that they were on private land. This feeling was soon replaced by certainty, when she saw that they were now entering a long drive surrounded by well-kept gardens. It could have been some exclusive country club of course, but the feeling that it was a private residence persisted in Cassy's mind. 'I hope it's not going to be a big party,' she commented to Sylvia, who was apparently lost in her own rosy world as she had not spoken for a few minutes.

Sylvia jerked out of her musings, and gave Cassy an apologetic look before she answered quickly, 'It's Justin's home,' adding hastily at Cassy's outraged gasp, 'At least, one of his homes.'

'I see,' said Cassy, tight-lipped, and glared at Sylvia.

'You knew I wouldn't have come if I'd known where we were going,' she said accusingly. 'I've a good mind to ask the driver to take me straight back to the hotel,' she added in a low vibrant voice.

Sylvia caught her arm. 'Please, Cassy, give him a chance,' she pleaded. 'It was his idea that we had dinner here, and that can only mean that he wants to apologise to you. Greg made me tell him the truth, and when he suggested that we had dinner with him— well, I could hardly refuse, could I?'

Cassy looked at her, and some of her fury dispersed; it wasn't Sylvia's fault that things had turned out the way they had. If only she had known their destination earlier, she would have worn something more appropriate, the skirt and blouse for instance, that Sylvia had spoken so disparagingly of. Oh, how she wished she had obeyed her instincts and changed before Sylvia had arrived! To turn up looking like this looked a little like great expectations, and Justin was bound to see it that way, but there was nothing Cassy could do about it now.

Justin was waiting for them by the arched doorway of a Spanish-style villa, dressed immaculately in evening wear, and Cassy's heart turned over as he approached them. She found it hard to meet his eyes, not quite knowing what to expect. His glance, and it was a glance, and nothing more, made her take a swift inward breath, since there was nothing apologetic in his manner, and certainly nothing to suggest that there was, or had been, anything between them.

Almost, thought Cassy, as if he was meeting her for the first time, and she was someone some friends of his had brought along to make the number up. There was also something a little condescending in his manner, that hurt her far more than a deliberate cold-shoulder attitude would have done.

It was as well for Cassy that Greg and Sylvia were in high spirits, and she was able to sit back and listen to the gay bantering going on around her. Sylvia was too much in love, and too preoccupied with her Greg, to notice that Cassy was being subjected to a cool dissecting appraisal whenever Justin looked her way, which he did fairly often, Cassy noted with high sensitivity.

When Greg had finished his digression on how he had won the tournament, not boasting, but purely for the benefit of an interested fellow golfer, the conversation turned to more personal issues, making Cassy wish uncomfortably that she had never left her hotel room.

Now that the tournament had finished, Greg would be off home again, but there were a lot of 'Ifs' and 'we'll sees' in the answers given, and a swift loving look in Sylvia's direction, that told its own story.

The dinner was excellent, at least, according to Sylvia and Greg, but for Cassy it was a case of getting through each course, all of which tasted like sawdust in her very dry mouth. For goodness' sake, why had Sylvia brought her here? She wasn't wanted, not by the fastidious man who sat next to her at the table, seeing to her wants as a nephew might see to the welfare of an extremely tiring aunt that he'd be glad to see the back of after the meal. If he felt that way, Cassy would have been only too happy to comply, but something told her he was not finished with her yet. In all probability he was saving up a lecture to be delivered as soon as they were alone.

That no such opportunity would present itself was a forlorn hope. Later they would stroll in the grounds, and Sylvia and Greg would wander off in the manner lovers usually did, leaving the apprehensive Cassy alone with Justin. She dropped her dessert spoon on the thought, and felt the heat rise up in her cheeks as she swiftly apologised for her clumsiness. Would this wretched dinner ever end? she thought miserably.

The dinner ended, but not Cassy's ordeal, for as far as she could see she had the worst part to come, and her steps dragged as she followed Sylvia out of the dining room and into a sumptuously furnished lounge for coffee and liqueurs.

All that Cassy had so far seen of the villa confirmed Sylvia's words that Justin Pride was a man of considerable fortune. Seated in one of the velvet-upholstered armchairs, Cassy tried not to look around her, but it was not easy, since Sylvia, having no such restriction placed upon her, openly admired the rich furnishings, and commented upon the gold-framed miniature paintings on the walls, all undoubtedly originals.

'Isn't that beautiful, Greg?' exclaimed Sylvia on spotting yet another treasure, this time an exquisite delicately engraved rose bowl displayed in a glass cabinet opposite them.

Cassy could have slapped Sylvia for her persistence in highlighting Justin's possessions, with so little regard to her feelings.

'Venetian?' queried Greg, after giving the bowl closer inspection.

Justin nodded. 'One of the finer pieces, I think,' he murmured.

Cassy, watching him and not looking at the rose bowl, saw the swift look he gave her before he answered. If she had been looking at the rose bowl, she would not have seen his glance rest on her before he replied to Greg's question. Was that why he had wanted her to come? she wondered. To show her that he was a man of substantial wealth, and how foolish she had been in turning him down? Was he trying to tell her she could have done very well for herself if she had agreed to his proposition?

Cassy's wondering eyes rested on him as he stood beside Greg and Sylvia holding the rose bowl in his long lean hands, and turning it slightly so that it caught the light and shimmered in a galaxy of rose-tinted rays. But it didn't make sense, she argued silently to herself as she watched him gently, almost reverently replace the bowl back into the cabinet. It might have made sense if Sylvia had not made her confession, but not now.

Coffee was then served to them by the same silent but very efficient manservant who had waited upon them at dinner, and sipping the Tia Maria that Justin had pressed upon them, Cassy realised with a sinking heart that they were about to embark upon the time that she most dreaded.

With a feeling that she was about to be thrown to the lions she heard Justin suggest a walk in the grounds, and heard Greg and Sylvia's almost relieved acceptance, understandable of course from their point of view, but pure panic from Cassy's!

Of course there had to be a moon, Cassy thought sourly, as they wandered down the terraces separated by rose-covered trellises, at least Cassy presumed they were roses purely by their rich scent, and although the light was good enough to show the way through the ornate garden, it was not good enough to identify the various blossoms whose perfumed aroma wafted around them.

Walking beside Justin, with Greg and Sylvia bringing up the rear, Cassy felt she was taking part in a play —a play she had suddenly been asked to perform in without proper preparation. She knew parts of it, but not others, and was not sure how good an actress she would turn out to be when the final curtain was lowered. She would either be a star or a failure. If Justin loved her, she would be a star—a star as bright as the ones now shining down upon them—but if he didn't, then she would vanish into obscurity.

All these thoughts went through her mind as she heard the questions put to Justin by Sylvia and Greg, such as how large the property was, and was that the Beach Hotel that they could see in the distance? All this she heard, yet none of it filtered through her haze of speculation. She only knew that she loved this man who walked beside her. Loved his deep well-modulated voice, loved the proud way he held his head as she watched him turn to answer yet another question put to him by Greg.

She was glad that she had worn this dress, she thought, as her fingers touched the soft folds of the material that whispered as she walked. It would always remind her of this night, of the bright moon and the dancing stars that attended it, the perfumed garden. Did Justin care for her? she wondered. He had been attracted, that much was certain. Had he wanted her there to prove to her that he was serious in his inter-

est in her? Her heart skipped a beat at the thought; it
could account for quite a lot of things that she hadn't
been able to understand. Was he afraid that she would
turn him down again, and was that why he had kept his
distance with her all evening? Try me and see, her
heart whispered silently to him.

She was so engrossed in her thoughts, she did not
realise that Greg and Sylvia were no longer following
them and came to with a start at Justin's smooth, 'We
seem to be alone.'

There had been a triumphant note in his voice that
Cassy took full note of. One could not say there was
anything loverlike in the tone, yet he swung round to
face her and pulled her into his arms, kissing her in a
manner that was both possessive and punishing.

'It's a pity to waste such a beautiful night,' he
whispered against her mouth, 'with such an entrancing
maiden, and I have no intention of letting such an
occasion pass.' His lips roamed her wide forehead, and
Cassy closed her eyes, but opened them wide at his
next remark. 'Particularly as we shall not meet again.
A pity, I feel, but you did rather underestimate me,
didn't you?'

Cassy blinked and came out of the euphoric state
that she had allowed herself to fall into, and as his lips
descended once more to claim hers, she twisted out of
his arms and stood looking at him. She could have
run away from him, but she needed to know why—
why he had hurt her so, and what he had meant by saying that she had underestimated him.

He smiled at her, and she caught the glint of his
white teeth. He held out his arms to her in a mocking
gesture. 'Come on, little spitfire, there's more to you

than meets the eye. Don't pretend you didn't enjoy my kissing you—your lips positively begged for more.'

Cassy remained standing where she was; once again he had made her feel cheap, and she wondered how she could ever have thought that she loved him. It was hardly gentlemanly of him to boast of his conquest, and still less gentlemanly of him to remind her that she had been a fool.

'Oh, well,' he said with a note of mock sorrow in his voice, 'I suppose we'd better go back to the villa. The young lovers will no doubt have pledged themselves to one another by now and will wonder where we've got to.'

With head held high, Cassy accompanied him back to the villa. Whatever he was now accusing her of she was not to know, it seemed, but it didn't matter now. Nothing mattered, except that she catch the first available plane back to the U.K. the next day. Back to sanity, since she was now convinced that these idyllic islands possessed some mysterious power that overrode all the normal reasoning processes.

Of Sylvia and Greg, she dared not think. Had they, too, been caught up in this nebulous fairyland? Well, at least she and Sylvia could console one another when sanity reigned once more, and at this thought she found herself having to stifle an hysterical chuckle.

There was still no sign of Sylvia and Greg when they got back to the villa, and Justin led Cassy into the lounge, and indicating that she should sit down, asked her with studious politeness what she would care to drink.

Cassy shook her head, answering in a low voice, 'Nothing, thank you,' then found she was totally unable to look at him and concentrated her gaze on one of the miniature paintings on the wall.

Following her glance, Justin mentioned the artist's name, but it meant nothing to Cassy, as she was not very well informed on the artistic front. Her total lack of interest seemed to infuriate Justin. 'It's worth quite a lot of money,' he told her, 'but I'm not concerned with material worth. Happily, I can afford to indulge myself.'

Cassy did look at him then; so she had been right in her earlier musings. He had wanted her there simply to show her that he was a wealthy man, and to rub in the fact that she had been stupid to turn him down. 'Bully for you!' she said in a light airy voice, thinking that she ought to have done better than that, but she was lost for words in the face of such blatant tactics.

Her light, unembellished answer infuriated him far more than a long bitter reproach on her part on his method of reprisal, for it was reprisal, Cassy thought, as she saw the fire in his eyes and a muscle jerk at the corner of his firmly set mouth. It was nice, she thought grimly, to be able to get a little of her own back.

She was not, however, allowed much time in which to savour her satisfaction, for he abruptly changed the conversation by commenting on her dress.

'It suits you,' he said in a silky voice, and his eyes narrowed as he surveyed its flimsy folds. 'Expensive, I'd say,' he went on smoothly. 'Part of the deal, was it?' he asked.

Cassy stared at him in puzzlement. What did he mean? What deal?

'You know, you should have stuck with Reggie,' he

commented idly. 'He might be past it himself, but he's still got some influential friends.'

Cassy was totally lost and looked it, and wished Sylvia and Greg would put in an appearance. She appeared to have lost part of the script in what was turning out to be the sort of play where you were left to make your own conclusions on the ending, and how she longed for the ending!

She glanced back at him, and saw that he was apparently waiting for an answer. 'I'll think about it,' she said lightly, matching his conversational tone, and darting a quick glance towards the open french windows that led directly on to the terrace.

'You do that,' he ground out, 'and while you're thinking about it, you might also consider another aspect—such as why you thought I'd be fool enough to fall for that story Sylvia came up with this morning.'

Cassy's eyes opened wide at this; so he hadn't believed her—no wonder he had treated her with such disregard!

'I might easily,' he went on grimly, 'have been hoodwinked, except for one rather obvious fact, and that was that no attempt had been made to straighten things out before. And that was odd, to say the least,' he added harshly.

Cassy still hadn't caught the trend of his thoughts, but afterwards she realised that she ought to have done. 'Before?' she echoed dully. 'Before what?'

'Before you became aware of my, shall we say, affluence?' he said meaningly.

No longer perplexed, Cassy gasped as the full implication of his meaning hit her. 'You think that I—

that we—that Sylvia and I . . .' She couldn't go on but stood staring at him wide-eyed.

'As I said,' he replied sardonically, 'you should have stuck with Reggie.'

Cassy's hands clenched into small fists and she leapt out of her chair as if propelled. She had had enough of this detestable man's company to last her a lifetime! 'I think I'll go and see what's holding Sylvia and Greg up,' she said haughtily, 'if you'll excuse me,' and began to walk towards the french windows, telling herself that they had had quite long enough to settle their affairs, lovers or no.

'You'll damned well leave when I'm good and ready!' Justin grated as he caught her arm in a steely grip and swung her round to face him. 'Let's have the gloves off, shall we?'

Cassy's right arm came up to slap his arrogant face so close to hers, but she was not allowed even this satisfaction as he caught her wrist before she had made contact with him and twisted her arm behind her back, forcing her struggling body to lie pliant against his hard frame, for his grip was painful.

'Shall I tell you what I think?' he said softly, his mouth only inches away from Cassy's bent head. 'I think you did a deal with Sylvia.'

Cassy could only shake her head wearily, for which she received a stronger grip and felt her cheek touch the soft material of his dinner jacket. 'You needed her co-operation, didn't you?' he went on inexorably. 'You'd decided to change horses in mid-stream, hadn't you? I think that's an apt description, don't you?' he purred. 'You promised to turn her father down if she'd help you to gain a richer prize—that's what it amounts to, doesn't it?' he said harshly. His fingers caressed her back and rested on the top of the dress, and she felt him grip the soft material hard in his steely fingers. 'She bought this for you, didn't she— as part of the bargain! You wanted to look good, didn't you?'

Petrified, Cassy felt his grip on the material tighten. 'Well, it didn't work,' he said savagely. 'You'll have no further need of such finery, it's hardly the type of dress you'd pick up in a village store, is it?'

'Oh, dear, have we come back at an inopportune moment?' queried Sylvia, amused. 'Shall we go out again, and come back later?'

As Justin's arms fell from her, Cassy moved swiftly away from his side thanking her lucky stars that Sylvia and Greg had arrived just in time to prevent him from tearing the dress to shreds. As it was, she wasn't sure how much damage had been done, for she had felt the material give way under his ruthless hands. 'No, please, it's all right,' she managed to get out, not caring if her voice did sound as panic-stricken as she felt.

'Well,' said Sylvia triumphantly, oblivious to the strained atmosphere between Justin and Cassy, and concerned only with her future. 'You may congratulate us! We're engaged!' she cried.

Cassy swallowed the impulse to shout back at them that they must be off their heads, and held out a hand that trembled slightly to Sylvia. 'Congratulations, dear,' she managed to murmur.

'And mine, too,' said Justin in what sounded like a normal voice, yet Cassy saw that his hands were clenched by his side. 'It appears that we have something to celebrate besides the championship,' and he strode over to the end of the room and pressed a switch and a miniature bar swung out silently from a wall niche.

'How the poor live!' commented Sylvia, not realising that she was rubbing salt into Cassy's wounds, and not seeing the quick sardonic look that Justin gave Cassy.

CHAPTER TEN

CASSY never knew how she survived the rest of that evening, but somehow she did, and somehow she managed to thank Justin for the dinner with studious politeness when they departed.

Had Sylvia not been so much in love, or so wrapped up in her future, she would have known that all was not well between Cassy and Justin. The same went for Greg, who was full of plans for the future, the first and foremost being to take Sylvia home with him the following day and introduce her to his parents.

As it was, Sylvia and Greg had presumed that they had walked in on a love scene between Cassy and Justin, and had no inkling of the true state of affairs, and the unhappy Cassy saw no reason to disillusion them.

The following morning Cassy wearily booked her passage back to the U.K. There was no point in staying on; she had lost all enthusiasm for further sightseeing, and only wanted to escape from the island that had caused her so much unhappiness.

Once she was home, everything would fall into perspective, she told herself determinedly. She might even be able to smile about her experiences, although the way she felt at that moment, that day was a long way away.

Sylvia rang her as she was starting to pack her suitcase, and she winced at the sheer exuberance of her tone. 'We're off at noon,' she told Cassy. 'I suppose you'll be staying the whole fortnight?' she said in an amused, knowing tone. 'Poor Dad,' she went on happily. 'Little did he know he'd lose the pair of us. I suppose it depends which one of us gets back first to break the news to him.' She gave a chuckle that made Cassy wince again. 'Anyway, I'll write to him as I promised, and tell him not to worry if he doesn't hear from you for a while.'

Cassy's hand gripped the receiver hard. As she was leaving precisely one hour after Sylvia and Greg, she would be home long before the letter arrived, and she knew she ought to have told Sylvia this, but she said nothing.

Mistaking her silence, Sylvia gave another chuckle. 'Hey, wake up, Cassy!' she teased. 'Shake some of that stardust out of your eyes.' Then she added, 'No, don't, it's a wonderful feeling, isn't it?' She sighed mistily. 'I'll leave you to your dreams. I promise to write and let you know about Greg's people. I only hope they take to me, I suppose it will be a bit of a shock for them. Greg marching in with his bride-to-be, I mean,' she added.

When Cassy was able to cut through Sylvia's meanderings, she assured her that she had nothing to worry about. She was sure that Greg's people would turn out to be very nice people, and if they were anything like Greg then they would be nice, and how she would look forward to hearing from Sylvia, ending with, 'Well, I'd better get on with my packing. I don't want to miss the booking I was fortunate enough to get at such short notice.'

'What booking?' demanded Sylvia sharply. 'Why are you going home? *Are* you going home?'

Cassy bit her lip in vexation. She was in a haze all right, but not the one envisaged by Sylvia. She frantically sought for some inspiration to cover her temporary lapse, eventually coming up with, 'Well, I've got to do something about the kennels, haven't I?' crossing her fingers in the hope that Sylvia would not seek further enlightenment.

'Oh, of course,' replied Sylvia, sounding relieved. 'For a moment I thought—yes, you'll have to straighten things out that end, won't you. Is Justin going with you?'

'No,' answered Cassy shortly. Not now, not ever!

'Oh, well, he's got so many business commitments, hasn't he?' Sylvia explained soothingly. 'But if I'm any judge of matters, he won't let you off the hook for long!'

She went on to give Cassy a message for her father, and after what seemed an age, Cassy was able to end the conversation.

At this rate, thought Cassy wretchedly, she wouldn't know truth from fiction. It only wanted Sylvia or Greg to run into Justin to blow the whole charade sky-high.

But how else could she have handled it? she muttered fiercely, as she threw her clothes into the suitcase. On no occasion had she had a chance to tell the truth. Then she frowned as she remembered the time when she had wanted to put Justin into the picture, and when Sylvia herself had wanted to own up.

She passed a hand across her forehead. On each occasion there had seemed a perfectly good reason as to why things should have been left as they were— either to protect Cassy from what she was convinced at the time was autocratic interference on Justin's part, and later his dubious attentions. Then there had been Sylvia to consider, and Cassy had been quite right in thinking that he would not have relished being made a fool of; his treatment of her had proved that beyond any doubt.

He was well named, she thought bitterly; it was pride that had made him act as he had. Not through any romantic or personal reason—pure pride had been his spur. He had wanted an affair with her and she had turned him down. She stopped packing and sat down on the bed. No little wonder he was so put out at Sylvia's disclosure. He hadn't wanted to believe her; hadn't wanted to admit that he had made a mistake in classing her as a gold-digger, and treating her as such by making that proposition to her.

Her soft lips twisted wryly. Poor Sylvia! In her eagerness to put things right, she had slightly overdone the explanation, and Cassy had to admit that it would have been hard enough for a man with much less reason than Justin Pride had to swallow the story.

With a sigh Cassy got up and re-started her packing. Oh, there had been reason enough to go through with it to the bitter end. What purpose would it have served if she had told Sylvia that her mission had failed so miserably? No purpose at all, Cassy thought grimly, except that of making Sylvia as miserable as she was, at a time when she should have been so happy. Eventually she would have to know, but not yet, and Cassy could always fabricate yet another plausible story as to why the so-called romance had failed. By that time Sylvia would presumably be arranging her wedding date, and engrossed with her own life.

As the plane soared off the runway right on time,

Cassy sat back and gave a sigh of pure relief, for she had been haunted with a fear that something would turn up at the last minute to prevent her from catching the flight. What, she had no idea—that either Greg or Sylvia would run into Justin perhaps, and that Sylvia would try to put the record straight before she left.

But all was well, she thought, as her eyes skimmed the skyline that was rapidly dwindling out of sight as the plane gained height. As well as it would ever be, she told herself sadly. Even allowing for the age-old proverb that the course of true love never ran smoothly, she hadn't stood a chance right from the start of her turbulent association with Justin Pride.

Cassy arrived at Heathrow in the early hours of the following morning, and booked herself into one of the nearby hotels. Now that she was home, there was no great urgency as to the time she arrived, particularly as she had not warned the family of her arrival, so she could return at her leisure.

The Surrey countryside looked green and fresh to Cassy as her train ate up the last few miles to her destination. Yes, she was glad to be home, she told herself, in spite of the ache in her heart whenever she thought of Justin, and Sylvia and Greg. Probably at that very moment Sylvia was meeting his parents, but Cassy had no worries on that score for her. It would be hard for anyone to take exception to Sylvia, she was so sweet-natured. Of course it would be a shock for Greg's parents, but after the first startling disclosure, Cassy was sure all would be well.

It was almost tea time by the time Cassy arrived back at Oaklands, the Mellar family home, and as she watched her cases being taken into the large roomy hall by the young cheerful taxi driver, she was grateful that her uncle would not be back from the City until six, giving her ample time to freshen up and prepare to bring him up to date with his daughter's affairs.

After she had showered, and changed into a light summer dress, she went in search of Christine, usually at this time to be found in the garden taking tea under the shade of the old oak tree on the edge of the lawn at the rear of the house. However, as she glanced towards the tree and saw no sign of her or any sign of preparation for a garden tea, she went to find Mrs Harland, the housekeeper, to see if she could enlighten her on this most unusual state of affairs, for Christine rarely absented herself from Oaklands. Even, thought Cassy, frowning, if she had presided over some village festivity, she always made a point of taking tea at home, extremely mindful of the fact that her new husband, should he take it into his head to return home earlier than his normal time, could be certain of her welcoming presence.

Mrs Harland was just on the point of going to the kitchen to make herself a pot of tea when she met Cassy in the hall. 'Why, Cassy!' she exclaimed in a voice that showed her pleasure at seeing her. 'When did you get back?'

'Not very long ago,' smiled Cassy, feeling a warm glow towards the housekeeper. At least she was pleased to see her. It was nice to know someone was! 'I've been looking for Mrs Mellar. She's all right, isn't she?' she asked.

Mrs Harland nodded quickly. 'She is, but her mother isn't so good,' she answered. 'But come on, I need a cup of tea, and I'm sure you do,' she shook her head in a sorrowful way. 'They can't make tea in those foreign places. You've probably forgotten what a good cup of tea tastes like.'

When the tea was made, Mrs Harland commented on Cassy's tan, that she said suited her, and that the holiday had obviously done her good, and how was Sylvia, and was she really going to stay out there? Knowing her of old, Cassy knew she would have to satisfy her curiosity before much progress was made in any other direction, such as why Christine was not at Oaklands.

Cassy replied to each question, giving only a slight nod to the 'you must have enjoyed yourself,' question —the least said about that the better! She told her of Sylvia's engagement to a well-known golfer, and warned her not to say anything about it until she had had a chance to tell Mr Mellar.

The delighted response this news produced slightly compensated Cassy for the delayed news she was waiting for, and she answered a few more questions as to how the romance started, and how soon she could expect to meet the future bridegroom, and would they be living in this country? The answer to the last question was almost certain to be no, but Cassy could only assume this; she did not know for certain, and said as much. It was a question of wait and see, but no doubt Sylvia would soon enlighten them on this.

After all this, Cassy had to remind Mrs Harland of her earlier quest. Where was Christine?

With a sigh of regret, Mrs Harland brought her mind back to what she would consider mundane affairs. 'She's had to go to Essex. Her mother's very poorly; she left yesterday, and doesn't expect to be back for at least a week. Mr Mellar,' she told Cassy with a gleam of irony in her eye, 'was very put out about it. Seems he's giving an important dinner on Friday.' She patted Cassy's hand. 'Still, he won't worry now that you're here,' she remarked complacently.

Back to square one, thought Cassy crossly, as she left Mrs Harland to her sentimental musings of orange blossom and rice. Trust her uncle to put his needs before those of others! In all probability Christine had been made to feel a traitor in leaving him at what he would consider an inopportune time! She was pleased that for once Christine had surprisingly stuck to her guns. Was the bid for the equality of the sexes making itself felt at last in the Mellar stronghold? First herself, then Sylvia, and now Christine! Poor Uncle George! Still, she mused, she could find time to arrange the dinner for him, as undoubtedly he would expect her to, but after that she would devote all her time to the kennels.

A glance at her watch told her that she had another hour to wait before she could expect to see her uncle, but Cassy could not wait that long before she knew for certain that the kennels were going to be hers. After collecting the present she had brought back for Mrs Peel, an ornamental brush set with mother-of-pearl backs, she slipped out of the house and taking her usual short cut through the back of Oaklands, made her way to the kennels.

Hearing the sound of excited barking and extra activity she knew that it was feeding time, and rounded the corner that brought her to the kennels expecting to see Mrs Peel in the thick of the activity. The activity was there all right, but not Mrs Peel; instead Cassy found herself looking at a middle-aged woman who had wrapped her hair up in a turban-like scarf and was shouting for someone called Arthur to come to lend a hand.

On catching sight of the surprised Cassy, the woman smiled at her. 'You're Cassy Aden, aren't you?' she asked. 'Enid told me you'd be around as soon as you got back. My, I must say I could do with some help, at that.' She stared at the pile of feeding bowls lined up in front of her, then did a quick count, and frowned in annoyance. 'Arthur, bring another two bowls, will you?' she shouted back at the still invisible Arthur.

Cassy knew she was expected to help with mixing the dogs' feed, but somehow her legs seemed too weak to comply with the action needed, for something told her that whoever this woman was, she was the new owner of the kennels.

'I'm Hilda Rose,' volunteered the woman. 'You'll be meeting my husband in a minute, if I can tear him away from that novel he's supposed to be writing,' she said, with an amused, indulgent smile. 'Enid said she couldn't have managed without your help,' she added, and Cassy wondered if this was meant to spur her into action, but still stood there. 'She's my aunt, you know,' she went on, now obviously a little puzzled by Cassy's inactivity, and the slightly stupefied expression on her face.

'Of course!' she exclaimed after she had given the matter a little thought. 'You wouldn't have heard. She was taken ill, you know. She hadn't been too good for quite a while, but I expect you know that. We had no idea that her health was so bad, and it was just as well for her that we were visiting at the time she collapsed.'

At Cassy's startled look, she hurriedly assured her, 'Oh, she's all right now, she just needs plenty of rest—no more of this work, though, so Arthur and I took over. She told us she'd been wanting to sell out anyway, since she'd found a place she wanted to buy.'

Cassy nodded. She couldn't think of anything to say. If she hadn't gone in search of Sylvia, she would have been on the spot when Mrs Peel collapsed, and she had no doubt at all that the kennels would now have been hers, instead of belonging to this stranger, even though she was a relative of Mrs Peel.

'Oh, Arthur, do get a move on!' shouted Hilda Rose, and cast an anxious glance at Cassy. 'You will come and help us out, won't you? Please do; there's lots we have to learn, and as you can see, my husband isn't exactly raring to go. He wasn't quite so keen on the idea as I was. He's just retired, you see, and I couldn't bear the idea of having him around all the time—not that I see him, if you know what I mean, he shuts himself in his study working on this book he's been threatening to write for years, but it leaves me entirely on my own, and I must do something.'

Cassy gave another brief nod, and wished she could think of something soothing to say, or at least promise to help out, but she desperately needed some soothing words herself. Not until then did she realise just how much she had been counting on the kennels, or ownership of the kennels, to help to erase her unhappiness. She had planned to throw herself into the work heart and soul, and not give one single thought to anything else. In the end she managed to say, 'I'm afraid I can't stop today, but I'll try and give you a hand whenever I can,' and on that flexible premise she left Mrs

Rose, still demanding her husband's presence.

When Cassy had got over her stark disappointment, she thought of her uncle. He couldn't have made the offer in time, for she could not see Mrs Peel allowing anyone else to take over, not if she had received a definite offer for the business. It all depended, she thought, on when Mrs Peel had collapsed, and by the sound of things it must have been shortly after Cassy had left for the Bahamas.

A lot, she thought bitterly, could happen in a few hours. If only Mrs Rose and her husband hadn't happened to visit on that day, and Mrs Rose hadn't had the brilliant idea of taking over. After a few seconds' thought on these lines, Cassy gave herself a mental shake. What was she thinking of! It was just as well that they were there to be able to help out—so in a way it was providence. Providential for Mrs Peel, bad luck for Cassy, who now wondered pessimistically if things would ever be right for her.

Her uncle viewed her return with a vast amount of relief—he was thinking of the dinner party, thought Cassy sardonically while she suffered a hearty pat on the back and a, 'Good girl, knew I could rely on you,' and went on to tell her about the trouble he was having with a few renegade shareholders. 'Think they've got me by the short hairs,' he said grimly, 'and there's been some offloading behind the scenes. Danielsson's want a merger, and if that's not on, they're preparing for a take-over.' He pulled at his lower lip. 'Mind you, there's something to be said for an amalgamation. The firm's steady enough, that's certain, and I'd keep control my end.'

Cassy listened, knowing there was no point in trying to divert the conversation back to a more personal one. As for the offloading of shares—well, she for one would seriously consider selling out to this Swedish firm if it turned out that her uncle had let her down over the matter of the kennels!

'I thought it might be a good idea if we all got round the table and thrashed the whole thing out,' went on her uncle, having no idea of the traitorous thoughts going through Cassy's head. 'And to that end I've invited them here for a conference. Dinner first, then we'll get down to business. That way it will remain confidential until a decision has been made, one way or the other. Danielsson's are in favour of this—they don't want a rush on the market any more than we do.'

After giving Cassy the list of guests expected, he added a jovial rider to the effect that if the dinner was up to her usual standard, he envisaged having no trouble with the ensuing business.

No mention of Sylvia, or Christine—or her mother's illness, thought Cassy wonderingly, for it never failed to surprise her that anyone could be so single-minded. 'Sylvia's engaged,' she said abruptly, thinking it was about time some other business was discussed, hers as well as Sylvia's.

He nodded complacently at this, and Cassy wondered if he had heard what she had said, but he proved that he had by showing her a cablegram. 'Sent me that yesterday,' he said, sounding pleased with himself. 'Had that fellow checked out by a golfing friend of mine. Seems he's heading for the big time.' He gave a hoarse chuckle. 'I'll have to polish up a few of my strokes, eh?' he commented to Cassy.

'What happened over the kennels?' she queried

quietly. He hadn't given a thought to her affairs, she thought bitterly.

He had the grace to look somewhat abashed at this. 'Sorry about that,' he mumbled. 'By the time I made the offer, it was all over. I acted as soon as I could,' he added quickly, on meeting Cassy's accusing eyes. 'When I went over there, the Peel woman was in hospital and two relatives had taken the business over. Er—there's a letter for you somewhere,' he frowned as he put his mind as to where he had left the letter. 'In the bureau in the lounge,' he said brightly, as if that would solve everything, and put things right. 'Er —from Mrs Peel,' he added helpfully.

Thoroughly disgusted, Cassy went in search of the letter. If she hadn't mentioned the kennels, it was doubtful if he would have remembered to tell her about the letter. Not that it would solve anything; the kennels were sold, but it might help her to understand why Mrs Peel had acted as she had.

Finding the letter, Cassy perused the contents in which Mrs Peel asked her to forgive her for what must have seemed a thoughtless action on her part in letting the kennels go to the Roses. Everything, she told Cassy, had seemed to happen at once. Her collapse, then a letter from the house agent telling her that the owners of the property she was interested in had had another offer and wanted confirmation that she was still interested. In other words, she told Cassy, they were not prepared to wait until she had sold her business. As she had sold the business to a member of her family, it had just been a case of transferring the property without the usual long legal wait, and she had been able to buy the cottage she had set her heart on.

She ended by telling Cassy not to be too down-hearted, and not to lose touch with the Roses, since she was convinced that given time, Hilda would lose her enthusiasm for the work entailed, particularly as she would have to play a lone hand in the business, for although agreeing to take it on, her husband had had certain reservations, but knew his wife well enough not to voice them.

What it amounted to, thought Cassy, was that Mrs Peel was telling her to bide her time, and in all probability her hopes of obtaining ownership of the kennels would be realised.

It was better than nothing, Cassy told herself; all was not lost yet, it was just a question of waiting. It was all very well for Mrs Peel to tell her to keep in close touch with the kennels, but if she did—if for example she carried on as before, taking on the lion's share of the work load—then it wouldn't be long before Hilda Rose was leaning heavily on her, not only work-wise, but experience-wise too. She had said that she had a lot to learn, hadn't she?

Cassy sighed deeply. She was in a cleft stick. If she stayed away, she would not be the first in line to take over the business. On the other hand, if she made herself indispensable, the chances were that the new owners would settle in comfortably. 'I'll think about it,' muttered Cassy to herself, and thrust the letter into her dress pocket.

By the time two days had elapsed, Cassy had made up her mind. She had the plans for the dinner on Friday well in hand, and as this presented no problem for her, she found time hanging on her hands. With all her spare time being taken up by the kennels in the past this was a new experience for Cassy, and one that she did not care for at all, since she was apt to find herself thinking about a certain tall man, with grey mocking eyes that seemed to continually haunt her solitude. As with the kennels, she needed time to get over that too, time to get him out of her system, and she wasn't going to do it by hanging around Oaklands.

There was only one solution. She needed work, and there was plenty waiting for her at the kennels. The following morning she presented herself for duty, and received such a fervent welcome from the exhausted Hilda that she was ashamed of herself for not putting in an appearance earlier.

By the time Friday dawned Cassy had a much clearer idea of what Mrs Peel had been trying to tell her, and had to agree with her assumption that Hilda's sudden decision to take over the kennels was not going to prove a very practical one. For one thing she had entirely forgotten to take into account the salient fact that the boarding kennels were at their busiest during the height of the summer season. As it was now the end of June, Cassy knew that the busiest time was yet to come, and when Hilda blithely told her that they were thinking of joining some friends of theirs in Monte Carlo for a few weeks at the end of July, adding with a smile that by then she would need a holiday, Cassy stared at her blankly.

'Were you thinking of getting someone in to look after the kennels?' she asked.

It was Hilda's turn to look blank now. 'But it will be August then,' she said, then frowned. 'I mean, we can't be expected to keep open all year round, can we?' she appealed to the surprised Cassy.

'Not all the year round, no,' replied Cassy gently, 'but August is the busiest time of the year for most kennels.'

Hilda stared aghast at her. 'Busier than we are at present?' she demanded incredulously.

Cassy nodded. 'I'm afraid so,' she answered, and nodded towards a low-slung building a few yards away from the main kennels. 'There's another ten boarding pens in there,' she told the gasping Hilda, 'and Mrs Peel was thinking of having the building enlarged to accommodate the overflow,' she added for good measure, thinking it was as well she knew what she had let herself in for.

'Overflow!' squeaked Hilda, pushing the inevitable turban further back from her head where it sat looking like a wispy crown on the top of her expensively permed hair.

'That's my girl,' said an amused voice behind them, and Cassy turned to meet the twinkling eyes of Arthur Rose. 'Having second thoughts, my dear?' he asked the floundering Hilda.

Hilda swallowed and gave her husband an exasperated look. 'I still think it's a good idea,' she said bravely, and looked back at the waiting Cassy. 'I told you we had a lot to learn, didn't I?' she said slowly. 'Does that mean that we don't get a holiday?' she asked in a slightly horror-stricken voice as she envisaged the future.

Cassy smiled at her. 'Oh, yes,' she replied, 'but you have to choose your time. January or February is usually a quiet time here, or just after Christmas,' she added after giving the matter more thought.

Hilda stared at her grinning husband. 'You can take

that grin off your face, Arthur Rose,' she said scoldingly, and sat down heavily on a side bench where they had been making out name labels for the next influx of boarders expected. 'We're both in this,' she reminded him.

'Oh, I don't know about that,' he replied in a mild voice. 'I did have a few reservations, if you remember,' he reminded her gently. 'If I remember rightly,' he said, gazing at nothing in particular, 'you did say that I didn't have to take an interest, and that you could manage. In which case I think I'll join Joan and Philip as previously arranged.'

'Arthur! You wouldn't go without me, would you?' appealed Hilda worriedly.

Cassy listened in some amusement to this exchange of wills between husband and wife. She had caught the slightly teasing quality of Arthur Rose's voice, and decided that she liked him very much. Hilda might think that she had affairs under control, but for all his quiet ways, it was her husband who really had the last word.

'Cassy? How would you like to become a partner in the business?' he suddenly asked the surprised Cassy.

Cassy looked from one to the other of them, not knowing what to say, and saw that Hilda was watching her husband with just as much curiosity. 'Why, I ...' she began, and looked back at Hilda.

Hilda smiled and nodded at her. She hadn't been married to Arthur for all those years not to know what was in his mind. 'Well? Why don't you?' she urged Cassy.

'Well,' gasped the still stupefied Cassy, 'I should love to become a partner—that's if you really mean it.'

'Oh, we mean it all right,' Arthur assured her firmly. 'The place was bedlam until you put in an appearance. We can see now just how much you helped Enid, without,' he added significantly, 'any remuneration.'

'Oh, well,' replied Cassy, embarrassed, 'it gave me something to do, and I loved the work.'

'Also,' Arthur went on firmly, 'I received strict orders from Enid that you were to have first offer at taking over should things not work out for us. I understand,' he added gently, 'that was what you hoped to do when Enid retired.'

'Arthur!' gasped Hilda. 'You didn't tell me this.'

Giving his wife a loving if slightly exasperated look, he replied gently, 'Would it have made any difference at the time, if I had? You know what you're like when you get the bit between your teeth. You would have accused me of trying to put you off, so I said nothing.'

Cassy was now horribly embarrassed and wished she could find some excuse to make herself scarce, but the labels had to be ready for the next day and she was only half-way through.

Sensing her embarrassment, Hilda smiled at her. 'Don't mind us, Cassy. Arthur's right as usual, and I am sorry I didn't know about your interest in the business—in taking over, I mean. I suppose I just thought you were amusing yourself with the work.' She gave Cassy an appraising look, taking in her slight figure in the well-fitting jeans and her simple blouse top, then her gaze rested on her slightly flushed face framed by her curly chestnut hair. 'It never occurred to me that someone like you would consider making the kennels a career. You're young and very pretty, and for goodness' sake what's wrong with the male popula-

tion around here?' she demanded. 'You ought to have
been snapped up long ago.'

Cassy's blush deepened, and Arthur coughed delicately. 'I think that's Cassy's business, Hilda, she's
probably not met the right one yet. Now, how about
a cup of coffee to celebrate the partnership?' he suggested lightly.

Cassy quickly volunteered to make it, and was able
to depart from what had been a heart-aching observation, albeit innocent, on Hilda's behalf. As for Arthur's
comment about her not meeting the right one—well,
she had—Justin was right for her, but she was wrong
for him.

CHAPTER ELEVEN

CASSY went back to Oaklands a little earlier than her usual time in order to start the final preparations for the dinner that evening. She knew she ought to have been overjoyed at the way things had turned out, yet somehow her spirits remained at a low level. Even the thought that it was now certain that she would be in sole possession of the kennels before much more time had elapsed failed to give her the uplift such news would have given her before her trip to the Bahamas.

Would it always be like this, she wondered miserably; had that one trip completely ruined her life? Only if she let it, she reminded herself firmly. Things had happened so fast, she hadn't had time to get herself acclimatised. In another week's time she would wonder why she had let herself get so low, and how stupid it was of her to moon over someone who didn't care one whit about her. Her pride would see to that, and she had no intention of falling into a well of self-pity—not for the likes of Justin Pride—or anyone!

Having decided that the best thing she could do was to put the past firmly behind her, and not allow herself the luxury of even one thought connected with a tropical setting, Cassy's strong resolve collapsed on sight of the beautiful amber dress hanging up in her wardrobe, as she searched for something to wear at the dinner.

Her eyes misted over as she touched the ripped portion of the zip at the back of the dress. Justin had wanted to destroy the dress, and had almost succeeded in doing so. It could be stitched up again, of course, but Cassy knew she would never repair it, for she would never wear it again.

She shook the wetness away from her eyes and continued with her search for something suitable to wear at the dinner, since her uncle had made her Christine's deputy for the evening. This task was not new to Cassy, she had acted as hostess on many occasions in the past before her uncle's remarriage, and had been only too pleased to pass on the duty to Christine.

It didn't really matter what she wore, she thought as her eyes passed over several dresses. It really only depended which dress was ready to wear without pressing, and she chose her apricot velvet. It always looked fresh, and the heavy velvet folds of the skirt never creased, making it an ideal choice.

When she was dressed, she went down to the dining room to see if the correct number of places had been laid, and to study the list of guests, for she would be expected to name each guest correctly as she circled the gathering in the lounge, serving drinks before dinner was announced.

The names of the Swedish contingent looked a little awe-inspiring to Cassy, and she hoped that she would be able to make a presentable stab at their pronunciation.

For a Mellar dinner party, it was a very small gathering; but that fact did not detract from the importance of the occasion, and Cassy knew that her uncle would expect a high standard, particularly in the cuisine line.

As she slipped through to the kitchen to have a

word with the cook, Cassy was grateful that she was not
expected to sit down to dinner with them, as Christine
would have done. Her role was simply to see that
everything ran smoothly, and that liquid refreshment
was continually on tap.

The fact that it was such a relatively small dinner
party presented no difficulty in the kitchen, and things
were well in hand by the time Cassy arrived, and all
she had to do was drift in, and out again, giving Cook
an airy wave of the hand as she left her to it.

Dinner was to be served at eight-thirty, and by eight
all the guests had arrived—at least all the guests who
were sitting down to dinner, but there would be another member of the Danielsson group who would be
joining them later in the evening to take part in the
business discussion following, and Cassy was directed
to watch out for his arrival.

The dinner went smoothly, and afterwards Cassy
passed the complimentary remarks on to a gratified
cook, and gave a sigh of relief herself. The business
part of the evening was about to begin and she could
bow out of the proceedings—at least, she could when
the Swedish contingent was complete. She glanced at
her watch and thought that it was about time the man
put in an appearance if he was coming.

As if on cue the front door bell chimed and Cassy,
giving a satisfied nod, went to answer the door.

The man swept in, and Cassy, not really looking at
him, directed him to the study, then realised that she
would have to have his name even though she had not
had a great success with the others, and turned to face
him as they reached the door of the study with a smile
of greeting on her face, a smile that froze into im-

mobility when she met the cold grey eyes of Justin Pride.

'You!' she whispered. 'What are you doing here?'

Justin's white teeth gleamed as he smiled back at her, although the smile did not reach his eyes. 'As Managing Director of Danielsson's, I'm expected to put in an appearance,' he answered laconically.

'I don't believe it!' gasped Cassy, although she did believe it. He was not the type of man to play games, not this kind of game anyway.

He stood there looking at her with one eyebrow raised, obviously waiting to be admitted into the study, and Cassy, looking quickly away from those mocking eyes of his, opened the door for him, but it was beyond her power to announce him.

It was a second or two before his arrival was noticed, as the men were in deep discussion, and Cassy, turning to make her departure, found her wrist caught by Justin's strong hand and held by her side, the folds of the dress hiding the action from observation. 'Which of those two old buffoons is it?' he asked her irreverently in a low voice.

Trying to disentangle her hand from his steely hold, Cassy saw that his malevolent gaze was on her uncle and old Mr Sanderson, his company secretary. 'If it's the one in the pin-stripe, I think I shall strangle you,' he went on in that sotto voce tone that only she could hear. 'I'll probably strangle you anyway,' he added softly, as his presence was suddenly spotted and he released her hand and moved forward into the room.

Bemused, Cassy heard the senior member of the Swedish team say, 'Glad you could make it; nice to have you aboard, sir,' as he shook his hand warmly, and Cassy closed the door with hands that trembled.

The thick fog that had descended upon her senses on sight of Justin simply refused to leave her and no amount of shaking of the head cleared it. How could he be Managing Director of Danielsson's and owner of several luxury hotels in the Bahamas? It didn't make sense, yet he had been recognised and warmly welcomed by Danielsson's directors. As improbable as it had sounded, he had told the truth—not that he had any reason to lie to her, but it did rather overreach the bounds of credulity.

Cassy stared at the lightly patterned wallpaper in her room as if she had never seen it before. Did Sylvia know of his connection with the Swedish firm? Then she shook her head slowly; even if she had done, she hadn't known about the latest developments, and if she had, it wouldn't have meant anything to her. Like Cassy, she had nothing to do with her father's business affairs.

She kept her mind running on this line of thought; it was safer than wondering just what was happening in the study, and fearing a sudden call for her appearance. She knew she would be expected to be on hand when the guests left, but she had no intention of budging from her room. She could always excuse herself afterwards by saying she had a headache—and this was not so very far from the truth, for her heart was palpitating at an alarming rate.

Although Cassy had gone to bed by the time the meeting broke up, she could not attempt to sleep until she knew Justin was off the premises, and waited until she heard the sound of motor car engines starting up outside the house. Only then did she feel that she could relax, for the time being anyway, but dreaded the following morning and the ensuing events of the meeting.

Coward-like, she kept out of her uncle's way the next morning, since as it was Saturday he would not be leaving for his office and would spend the day at home.

Cassy did not know what she would have done if she hadn't been able to escape to the kennels, and she made certain that she was there long before her uncle put in his appearance for breakfast, even though he was an early riser.

As she exercised the dogs that morning, Cassy found that though she could keep herself busy, she could not stop the events of the previous evening from dominating her thoughts. She badly wanted to know the outcome of the talks; if they had agreed to amalgamate, and would that mean that Justin would make spasmodic visits to Oaklands. What about the hotel business? Did he intend to sell up and settle in the U.K.? At this thought Cassy's small white teeth bit into her soft lower lip; she would far rather he stayed in the Bahamas. She didn't want to see him again, she wanted to forget his very existence, but he didn't appear to be exactly co-operative in granting her this wish.

There was one other thought at the back of her mind that kept recurring with depressing regularity; what if Justin was set on revenge? He'd said something about strangling her if it was the man in the pin-striped suit, and it had been! Was he just being facetious at her expense? All reason pointed to that explanation, yet she could not rid herself of a feeling that there was a little more to it than that. Why had he bothered to put in an appearance, to come all that way just to clinch a deal, unless he had an ulterior motive? It was this ulterior motive that worried Cassy.

After all the dogs were exercised, Cassy left Hilda to it, saying that she would be back later to help with the feeding. The bulk of the work had been done by then, and she could leave with a clear conscience, since now that she was a partner in the business she was under an obligation to give a helping hand.

Normally Cassy would have stayed all morning at the kennels, finding work to do, for there was always something that needed attention, if not taking bookings, collecting the dogs from the pens when their owners called for them, particularly the latter at the weekends. Today, however, the kennels took second place in her thoughts; she had to know the outcome of yesterday's meeting, and couldn't bear the suspense any longer.

It was eleven o'clock by the time she arrived back at Oaklands, and expecting to find her uncle in the study, she made her way there as soon as she entered the house.

The sound of voices did not deter her from opening the door and going in. Her uncle usually had a session with a man from the village who pottered about in the garden during the week, and Cassy was sure of the identity of her uncle's visitor.

A second later she was backing out of the study with flushed cheeks, for Justin Pride and her uncle were having what could only be described as a business conference.

'Don't go,' drawled Justin, his eyes lingering on her bright cheeks. 'We've settled our business, and I think we've both had enough for one day.' He glanced at George Mellar with a lifted eyebrow, seeking confirmation on this point.

Her uncle nodded his head. 'Most satisfactory,' he said in a pleased tone. 'And now,' he added as he got up and looked at Cassy, 'I must go and collect Christine. You didn't tell me you'd met Mr Pride in Nassau,' he accused her lightly, 'and I must say I was surprised to find that you'd gone off to those kennels this morning, particularly as Mr Pride is staying for the weekend.' He cleared his throat importantly. 'Still, you can make up for your absence by entertaining him for the rest of the day. I don't suppose we shall be back before six.'

Indignantly Cassy looked at her uncle; he hadn't told her that Justin Pride was a house guest, although she would have known, she thought guiltily, if she hadn't bolted up to her room and stayed there. She knew Justin was watching her closely and that made things worse for her. 'I'm not sure Mr Pride would welcome my company for the rest of the day,' she said crossly, not liking the way her uncle had foistered his company on her.

'I'm very much looking forward to it,' commented Justin in a firm voice that told her that she wasn't going to get out of this obligation.

'Well, that's settled then,' commented her uncle before Cassy could add her sentiments on the matter, and strode out of the room. A few seconds later the sound of a car starting up and wheels crunching down the drive told Cassy she was on her own, and there was a hint of panic in her eyes as she met Justin's amused ones.

'I'm glad you're amused,' she said coldly. 'And I

can't think,' she added furiously, 'how we're expected to fill in the rest of the day.' Her eyes fell on the pile of papers on the desk. 'Why don't you have another business conference with your colleagues? You must want to get everything straight before you go back,' she snapped.

'You are in a prickly mood, aren't you?' replied Justin softly. 'I think perhaps I can do something about that. Come here, Cassandra,' he ordered autocratically.

Cassy's heart turned over. He was so sure of himself, wasn't he? In a day or two's time he would be off to the other side of the world, leaving her to pick up the pieces. Well, there weren't going to be any pieces. She wasn't going to get caught like that. 'Would you like to see the garden?' she asked, ignoring his command.

His quick drawn-in breath told her that he hadn't liked the change of conversation, if one could call it that, and his voice left her in no doubt. 'Later, perhaps,' he answered abruptly. 'When we've got a few things straightened out.'

Cassy looked at him, her lovely blue eyes echoing her thoughts as she said clearly, 'We've nothing to straighten out. Sylvia lied to you, and I had to back her up.' Her voice was bitter as she added, 'I don't blame you for not believing her when she tried to tell you the truth. It must be difficult for someone like you to understand that there are other motives for such actions, apart from monetary ones.'

He was silent for a moment or so, then said quietly, 'I suppose I asked for that, but I didn't come halfway across the world simply to find out the truth.'

Cassy's hands clenched into small fists. No, he hadn't been able to resist dragging the saga on. 'Of course you didn't,' she replied tightly. 'You came to put your signature on the dotted line, if Mellar's were willing to play ball—which apparently they were,' she added viciously, and glared at him. 'I also suspect that you couldn't resist taking a look at the man you thought I'd turned you down for. I'm right, aren't I?' she demanded furiously.

'Partially,' he said casually. 'Not wholly.' He thrust his hands in his pockets and turned to look out of the study window and across the lawn. 'I did want to see the man you appeared to want to sell yourself to, but it was more than that. I had to make sure that Sylvia had told me the truth this time, and if not,' he looked back at Cassy, 'I intended to break Mellar.'

Cassy's eyes opened to full capacity. 'You're not serious!' she cried, imagining her uncle in a broken heap on the floor.

Justin's eyes travelled slowly over her face before he answered quietly, 'That too, probably, the way I felt. In reality, however, I mean financially. And I could have done it, too; we've enough shares in the Company to swing things our way. As it happened it wasn't necessary—we've amalgamated.'

Gasping, Cassy was about to fall back on her favourite, if well worn phrase, that she was apt to use when utterly confused, 'Bully ...' was as far as she got, for the next moment she was in Justin's arms and being kissed in no uncertain fashion.

When he lifted his lips from hers a moment later, he murmured softly, 'If you say, "Bully for you," to me once more I shall thrash you,' he threatened her lovingly.

There was no need for her to ask him if he loved her,

it was there in his eyes, in the possessive way he held her as if frightened to let her go, and he said so. 'You're not doing the disappearing act on me again, my girl,' he muttered as his lips roamed her forehead. 'When I phoned the hotel the next day and found that you'd left for home, I was desolate; I knew then without a doubt that I loved you to distraction, and the thought of you winging your way back to a man old enough to be your father tortured me. I cursed myself for not handling things better. That day I came to your hotel room, for example, I ought to have made my intentions quite clear to you. I ought to have proposed to you—in a way I was proposing, but you failed to see it that way.'

He kissed a wayward curl that had strayed across her forehead. 'When I'd calmed down and gone over that scene in my mind, I realised what a mess I'd made of the whole affair.' He looked down at her now pliant in his arms. 'You were right, my love, when you said it was difficult for someone in my position to understand any other motive but a mercenary one. I learnt a long time ago how to distinguish friends from hangers-on, and there were always plenty of those. I also learnt never to take anyone at face value, but to make my own judgments.' He sighed. 'And this I did with you; no matter how I tried I simply could not see you as a grasping siren. I think I must have fallen in love with you straight away, although I hadn't realised it. I only knew I wanted to be with you, but you kept turning me away.'

Cassy's arms went up around his neck as he said this, and she clung tightly to him. 'I thought you were only playing with me,' she whispered against his lapel.

'Not at first,' he said softly, 'but afterwards, I must confess some such ploy did enter my mind, particularly as you'd made it clear that you were only interested in money, and that you thought you'd be wasting your time with me.' He gave her a little shake. 'Beachcomber, indeed!' he said scoldingly. 'I'd never given it a thought,' he went on musingly, 'that anyone could be ignorant of my affluence, and I must admit that Sylvia's confession came right on cue, as it were. It seemed obvious to me that you'd made a few enquiries about me, and must have received a shock. I reasoned that you would attempt to repair the damage, and that's precisely what I thought Sylvia's disclosure was in aid of. When you arrived that night looking like a wood nymph in that floating amber thing, I wanted to strangle you. You looked so lovely that I wanted to hurt you as much as you were hurting me.'

His lips twitched as a thought struck him. 'I suppose I ruined it, didn't I? I suppose if Sylvia and Greg hadn't made their appearance right then, I would have torn it from your back, I was so beside myself.'

Cassy looked up at him with a twinkle in her eyes. 'The zip's a bit askew,' she said softly, 'but it can be repaired, I think.'

'I'll buy you another,' he replied gently. 'Several, in fact. I like you in that colour.'

Later as they walked through the garden hand in hand, Cassy realised there were still a lot of things she didn't understand, such as the fact that Justin owned Danielsson's.

'My father's business, actually,' he explained, after she had put the question to him. 'I inherited it after his death two years ago. My interests lay in other directions, and I was quite happy to leave the firm in the hands of the management that had run it in my father's time. Of course,' he said on a note of amusement, 'I was informed of any big decisions, and asked to provide my comments, but by and large I never interfered —except on this one occasion.' He squeezed her hand. 'Ironical, wasn't it, that they should have had their sights set on your uncle's business. International Trucking didn't mean a thing to me, that was the name that came through with their communications with me. It was only when I made a few enquiries about the Mellar business that I realised that International Trucking was his business, so I told them to hold everything and wait for me to join them.'

Cassy was silent for a while, then she asked, 'Would you really have ruined poor Uncle George?'

He swung her round to face him. 'What do you think?' he said softly. 'If you wanted a rich man, then you'd get a rich man, but it was going to be me. This time I wasn't going to take no for an answer.'

Seeing the determination in those grey eyes of his, Cassy's eyes misted over. 'I love you,' she said softly. 'I loved you as a beachcomber, too,' she added, and would have said more, but his fiercely possessive arms closed about her, and his hard demanding lips, effectively curtailed the rest of the sentence.

JOY ROMANCE LOVE

Harlequin Omnibus

THREE love stories in
ONE beautiful volume

The joys of being in love...
the wonder of romance...
the happiness that true love brings...

And there's still *more* love in

Yes!

Six more spellbinding
romantic stories every month
by your favorite authors.
Elegant and sophisticated tales of
love and love's conflicts.

Let your imagination be swept away to
exotic places in search of adventure,
intrigue and romance. Get to
know the warm, true-to-life
characters. Share the special
kind of miracle that
love can be.